Af

Brandon Shire
Copyright © 2012 Brandon Shire

This novel contains adult content and is intended for mature readers over the age of eighteen.

All rights reserved. Without limiting the rights under copyright reserved above, no part of this publication may be reproduced, stored in or introduced into a retrieval system, or transmitted, in any form, or by any means (electronic, mechanical, photocopying, recording, or otherwise) without the prior written permission of both the copyright owner and the below publisher of this book. This is a work of fiction. Names, characters, people, places, schools, media, incidents and events are either a product of the author's imagination, or are used fictitiously.

ISBN 13: 978-1480289819
ISBN 10: 1480289817

Special thanks go to

Blind LGBT Pride International

They helped keep things accurate and gave me information to dispel some of the myths surrounding blind people in general and gay blind people in particular.

Any mistakes are my own.

Author's Note:

This novel contains graphic depictions of unsafe sex. The author neither condones nor encourages this type of behavior.

You should always practice safe sex.

Afflicted

Brandon Shire

What are readers saying about Brandon Shire's books?

Listening to Dust

A gay love tragedy between a young American soldier and an English writer, and how homophobia ripped them apart forever.

"Best in LGBTQ Fiction for 2012" – Indie Reviews

"A haunting story by a master storyteller."
- *The Wilde Writers Collective*

"Beautiful, stunningly beautiful."- *Joyfully Jay Reviews*

"Will break your heart into pieces." – *Bittersweet Reviews*

"Shire is a master with words... This book is an absolute must read." – *Chapters & Chats*

The Value of Rain

The story of a boy institutionalized for being gay and his quest for revenge when he is finally released.

'Best in LGBTQ Fiction for 2011' – Indie Reviews

'Top Read of 2011' – The Reading Life

Afflicted by love's madness all are blind.
-Sextus Propertius

Chapter 1

Hunter knew this wasn't one of those childish boy-whores trolling for perverts. This was a man. He was young, but still a man. Being blind, Hunter couldn't see him, but the timbre of his voice spoke of mystery. Someone who'd done things which he'd never acknowledge. A man who'd lent himself to situations where his precociousness couldn't have extracted him safely, yet he'd gone anyway. Had it been for the money? Or the drugs? Or just for the thrill? Hunter wasn't entirely sure, but he planned to find out.

The man had a hard street smell to him – the coarse weave of slightly greasy jeans; the soft, worn odor of a leather jacket; the musty, unwashed smell of lank hair. What would his feet be like trapped in boots all day? Not rank, no. They might have a slight vinegar smell, like chips, only with a more sensual under-tongue taste.

And what would he feel like up close? It was so hard to tell by the sound of his voice. Hunter tried to picture him.

Maybe his mouth was fleshy and full – drawn cheeks buttressing a square chin; a sinister, almost cool-sly secret smile hinting at the exciting mysteries of his flesh. The nose might be proud, Romanesque; or maybe buttoned up small, like a child's – somehow lending innocence where there wasn't any. His eyes might be slightly pretentious – the slitted, oval shape of some Asian ancestry; or maybe he had the round, bedroomed look of some high European lineage.

And what of his poise? Was it haughty? Did he hold a mild distance, unerringly begging you to pull him in close? Did he burn you with a cool, liquid stare that dried the mouth? Or did he bark a seductive, fuck me trash-boy look meant to melt the eyes?

"All right, sorry," the man said as he started to walk off. His voice was low, but solid, melting, and caramel smooth. It wasn't foreign, but had a rough edge to it as if he'd been suppressing the roll of his R's all his life in some small Southern town.

Curious, Hunter speculated about whether the enunciation was purposefully false – something he used to keep potential customers guessing. "Okay," Hunter called out, making sure he was loud enough to halt the man's retreat.

His leather jacket creaked as he slowly turned to eyeball Hunter once again.

What did he see that made him ask? Hunter wondered.

He lit a cigarette that was so obnoxious it had to be foreign. Hunter sniffed. "Dunhills?"

"Rothmans," he answered. There was a smile in his voice. "Have you ever done this before?"

"Have you?" Hunter replied, his tone mildly defensive.

"Every day," he answered casually, a swagger in his voice that wasn't quite as triumphant as his words were meant to be.

"With a blind man?" Hunter queried.

"Mm, no, I admit it's a first."

There was another smile there too, but his response hadn't seemed wholly truthful. It made Hunter pause, but he quickly thrust his concerns aside. "That makes two of us, come on."

As he fell in beside Hunter, the scent of lotion tickled at Hunter's his nose. The guy was waving his hand in front of Hunter's face to see if he was really blind. Apparently, the red-tipped cane hadn't clued him in enough. Not good. "What's your name?" Hunter asked as if oblivious.

"Frank. Yours?"

"Is that your real name?"

"Are you going to give me yours?" Frank countered playfully.

Hunter smiled and wondered just what the hell he was doing. This was so dangerous. Anything could happen and he'd never be able to identify the guy after.

In an hour, he could be bleeding in a hospital bed trying to tell the cops what Frank sounded like. They'd shake their heads at his stupidity and offer false assurances that he'd be found, even though everyone would've already understood the impossibility of the task.

But the sexual energy of this potential escapade was already making Hunter's prick stiff with longing and lust, and nothing would likely change his mind now that Frank was by his side.

"You know the neighborhood," Frank observed as they walked.

They'd crossed through an intersection and Hunter took note of the fact that Frank hadn't tried to "guide" him to the opposite sidewalk.

Frank was off to a much better start than he realized. Six months ago, some idiot trying to be a Good Samaritan had seized Hunter's arm without even asking if he needed help, which he didn't. It had taken every ounce of Hunter's self-discipline not to cuss the guy out and beat him to a pulp with his cane.

"Enough to get home, but I usually drive through," Hunter answered.

Frank took a minute before he laughed, not quite sure if it was supposed to be a joke.

"No, really. I had an argument with a friend earlier. I told her to fuck off and decided to walk home when she finally stopped the car."

"That must have been some argument," Frank said, phrasing it as more of a question than a statement.

Hunter said nothing because it had been a ferocious quarrel with his friend and co-worker, Margie. Margie was great, but she had a bad habit of questioning Hunter's need for independence. Their words had been bitter enough that he honestly wasn't sure if their friendship would survive.

"You didn't tell me your name," Frank said.

"Hunter."

"Say again."

"Hunter, as in a man chasing defenseless animals with a too

powerful weapon," Hunter told him. "It seems a little ridiculous for a blind man, but…" He shrugged. "There it is." He stopped suddenly and listened as Frank stopped beside him. "Tell me what you see," he instructed Frank. "What do you see?"

Frank was quiet for a few seconds, apparently trying to gauge his question.

Hunter let the silence hang between them as a dapple of sunlight warmed his face – this meant the trees he heard whispering in the breeze were likely right overhead. He tilted his face to the heat in delight and took a deep breath.

"A deep green melancholy," Frank finally answered.

Impressive, Hunter thought, and definitely not what he'd expected to hear. Was it their surroundings, or what he saw in Hunter that elicited such a response?

Hunter started walking again but purposefully faltered his step to see if Frank would reach out and try to save him from falling. He did.

Hunter felt the firm, resistant flesh of Frank's palm on his arm almost immediately. His fingers cupped Hunter's elbow, his nails scraped lightly against his skin. Fast, firm grip and he has some strength.

"Why did you explain it like that?" Hunter asked as they paused again, the scurry of busy squirrels chattering overhead.

He sensed a shrug as Frank released his arm. Cigarette smoke rushed by even as Frank attempted to blow it in the opposite direction.

"It's true," Frank answered.

"Explain it. Give me the details," Hunter urged him. He'd actually asked the question to see if Frank was a fucking moron. He didn't like to lay claim to being conceited, but common sense and the ability to communicate beyond the bedroom were pretty high on Hunter's list of must-haves, even for a male prostitute.

Frank inhaled deeply on his cigarette, and then exhaled another burst of obnoxious smoke as he collected his thoughts. "The road is still shiny and wet in splotches from the shower that came through earlier," he said after a moment. "You can probably smell the water evaporating up off the tar. Otherwise the neighborhood looks, on the whole, dull and cracked and gray. There's a yellow tomcat sitting on the corner preening itself while he soaks in the sun and watches traffic go by. He doesn't seem as concerned about us as the guy trying to hide himself behind the soaped-up window of that little bistro they're finishing across the street."

"What's the bistro look like?" Hunter interrupted.

Frank paused, collecting his words again. "I think it might be interesting if they ever get it open. The building has a new brick facade on the front with dingy cinderblocks making up the other three sides. But it has a nice patio. Across the street, there's a bookstore that smells of ink and coffee and new pastries. But you know that already."

Hunter smiled because he did know that intermixed fragrance of books and pastries. It was one of the aromas that helped him navigate. He could always tell where he was on this corner by how strong it was.

Frank paused for a moment longer and Hunter assumed he was looking around, readjusting his observations.

"It almost seems like the whole corner is trying to come alive again, but at the same time avoid the clichés that would make it haughty. Some iron railings and these old oak trees and it might work for one of those old village concepts they seem so fond of these days," he opined before he took another drag. "How was that?" he asked as he turned back to Hunter.

"Good, except for the colors, I don't have a reference for them. Do you write?" Hunter asked as they started toward his apartment again. "Your description was…interesting."

Hunter felt him shrug through his voice again. "I can see more details than I could put on paper with any flair. You live far?"

"No, down the street, one block over." Hunter could hear the pity in Frank's words before he even spoke them.

"You do know the area well," Frank said, omitting the for a blind guy part.

But Frank's tone didn't contain the pretentious pity Hunter typically got from sightlings. It held something different, something a little deeper than the shallow misconceptions of the sighted. It made Frank stand out a bit more.

"Well enough to know that you aren't usually here," Hunter quipped. In fact, he knew the area very well. He'd spent weeks exploring it with a seeing guide before he struck out on his own. At the time, he'd been determined to be familiar enough with his neighborhood that he wouldn't be dependent on anyone. Nothing irked him more than asking for help for something as simple as grabbing milk from the grocery store.

"I wasn't really..." Frank's voice faded in distraction or shame. Hunter wasn't sure which.

"You weren't really what?" Hunter pushed. He'd lived in Atlanta for seven years and this was the first time he'd ever been approached by a male prostitute. Honestly, it felt pretty damned good.

"I wasn't working," Frank answered. "I was just feeling out the neighborhood."

"Reconnaissance for some new turf?" Hunter asked, a coy smile lifting the corners of his mouth.

The smile came back into Frank's voice. "Apartment hunting."

"I think you'd like the neighborhood, but I don't know if the homeowner's association would be so gracious about you hanging out on the corner."

Frank laughed, it was a gentle sound. Hunter knew he'd like to hear it more often.

"I don't hang out on street corners." Frank chuckled. "But I do like to walk a neighborhood before I move in. You can get a better feel for it than if you just drive through."

Hunter nodded in agreement, but then he wondered why Frank had hit on him if he was just looking for an apartment. It was relatively early in the evening, and he was blind. And, to be honest, it was pretty ballsy to be accosting a blind man on the street for sex.

But the more he thought about Frank's proposition, the more he said why not? Why wouldn't Frank approach a blind man? Hunter was just as horny as any other man, and he liked sex and he had money, so why not? It wasn't like he had men lining up with offers.

He stopped again. "Can I… touch you?" This was not something he, or any other blind person, normally did to a stranger. But if Hunter was going to take Frank home to bed, he had to know.

"Out here? In the street?" Frank asked scandalously. "Do you want to get us both arrested?"

Hunter laughed. "You know what I mean."

Frank's voice got quiet. "Yes, I do."

He took a step closer. Hunter could feel the heat from his body and smell the underlying aroma of power and masculinity. He ran a hand over Frank's chest, his solid pecs, and his six pack abdomen. He wanted to slide his hand around and see if his ass matched the rest of him, but Frank was right. That kind of exploration would be better done in private.

"Do I pass?" Frank asked, whispering in his ear, his voice husky.

Hunter ran his hand across Frank's broad shoulders, around the curve of his neck, down his square jaw. Frank nipped at his fingers as they went by, causing him to smile.

Frank's arms were thick and sturdy, but polite – not secure, but patient, an endemic quality of his trade, Hunter guessed. His neck and chest were formal, diligently cut and sculpted with muscles to be candy for the eye, a sweet Hunter could not taste as a blind man.

Hunter bit his lower lip. He really wanted to see how Frank was hung, but if it measured up to the rest of him…

Oh, yes. He passed all right. "Did I tell you my apartment is right around the corner?" Hunter asked.

Frank laughed.

Chapter 2

Dillon's eyes popped open. He was still in Hunter's bed. The sun hadn't risen yet, but this was normal. Physically, his body was used to the schedule and he woke automatically, whether he wanted to or not. But unlike most of his other working mornings, he wasn't mentally ready to depart yet. He actually wanted to stay.

One of the charms he used on his clients was to always rise extra early and leave before they awoke. He left them with the residual, and in their words, mystical aura of whatever proclivity they'd paid him for. Some clients wanted hard lust, others needed passionate romance, and a few just sought out the radiant heat from his body. But always, when they awoke in the morning, he was gone.

But when he woke up beside Hunter, he suddenly didn't want to leave. He had to pull his hand back from an involuntary urge to reach out and caress Hunter's jawline. He didn't know Hunter at all, yet, last night, unexpectedly, he'd had the urge to divulge his real name and stay until Hunter woke up.

Maybe he'd watch from the bed while Hunter shaved and got ready for work. He could already see them having breakfast together…

Where is this shit coming from? he asked himself. He lay propped up on one hand watching Hunter sleep. His brow furrowed.

Dillon, his real name, hadn't propositioned a trick since he was nineteen and regained consciousness behind a dumpster after being beaten, robbed, and dosed with GHB. At the time, he couldn't remember much more than how much his body hurt. Since then, he'd started working for an agency. The incident had broken him of the habit of street-corner soliciting permanently. At least he'd thought so, until now.

So what had it been about Hunter that intrigued him? What had stopped him dead cold on the street and pulled a proposition straight from the pit of his gut? Hunter was hot, that was easy to see. Dillon had no doubt Hunter was sought after, even if Hunter couldn't see for himself that he was some serious eye candy. He had to know it by the interest he received, didn't he? Weren't there subtle, flirty communication cues blind people used?

And yet, Hunter had seemed surprised at Dillon's interest. So maybe he wasn't getting the attention he deserved. Dillon knew how pretentious the queens of this city could be. They were always chasing some idea of perfection – the perfect car, the perfect job, and the perfect man to round out their perfect look.

Funny how many never found it. Then, when they failed to figure out why they were alone all the time, they fell into drink, drugs, and ruin. He'd seen it so many times that he wanted to slap some of them and tell them to wake the fuck up.

He specifically recalled how one of his old clients had taken him out to dinner, boasted loudly about everything he'd done on his recent and extravagant trip to Miami Beach, and then embarrassed himself by offering one maxed-out credit card after another to pay their small dinner tab. The whole night was supposed to have been a grand show for the benefit of the other restaurant patrons. In the end, Dillon had paid for their date and then dumped him from his client roster just for the embarrassment he'd caused.

But that had nothing to do with the man who lay in front of him. If anything, Hunter seemed the exact opposite from that eager, boastful jackass.

So now what? he asked himself as he watched Hunter's chest rise and fall.

If he was honest, he didn't really know why he'd propositioned Hunter. It just kind of happened, and he was just as shocked as Hunter seemed to have been.

But last night was the first time he hadn't faked sex in… Hell, he couldn't even remember when that was. He'd wanted Hunter from the second he saw this dark-haired god on the street. And, he wanted him more when they got back to the apartment and got Hunter's clothes off.

Hunter was hot. He was solid and muscled and had a cock on him like a stallion. But there was more to him than that, and it was something Dillon felt immediately.

His eyes ran down the contours of Hunter's sheet-covered body.

He hadn't mentioned it, but after accompanying so many bodies between the sheets, he knew there was no way Hunter could have a body like this if he weren't working out somewhere. His hands were hard like they were grasping iron rods all day, and his muscles were taut but flexible. It was odd because he didn't have a body like a gym rat. He had a body like an athlete's — toned, muscular and exquisite. And when he'd turned around and pushed his ass back at Dillon… Man, it had taken all of Dillon's reserve not to rip his condom off and breed Hunter right there on the spot. He was breathtakingly beautiful.

He let out a long, appreciative breath and adjusted himself now that he'd gotten all worked up again. He slipped out of the bed without making any noise. While he put his clothes on, he watched Hunter sleep, brooding about how it would feel to wake up next to someone like him. Maybe he wouldn't feel like an accessory any longer. Maybe he wouldn't feel…disposable.

He'd been speculating about that more and more lately. But he couldn't decide if it was the new circumstances of his life putting the thoughts into his head, or the fact that he was just getting bored with all the bullshit of hustling his ass. It wasn't just unsafe anymore; it was tiresome – emotionally, physically, and financially. He didn't need to hustle any longer, but what else was there?

He picked up the clothes they'd thrown off, folded Hunter's neatly on a chair, and then paused as he stared at the money on the dresser. Still a little lost as to whether he wanted to take it, he glanced back at Hunter. There was so much implication in not taking it, and yet so much finality in completing the transaction.

Finally, he scraped the bills into his pocket and slipped out of the bedroom. Despite his early morning fantasy, that's exactly what this was: a transaction. One that he'd conducted hundreds of times before.

He walked to the front door and smiled as his eyes flicked to the bathroom. Hunter hadn't wanted him to shower. He'd wanted him funky and street raw. That little twist of kink had made Dillon rock hard in an instant simply because it was so different from the manicured candy his clients usually paid for. Unfortunately, he'd been so funky from walking that he couldn't stand himself and had to grab a quick shower so he could enjoy their time too.

Maybe next time, he thought as he closed the door and slipped from the apartment.

If there was a next time.

Chapter 3

The heat of the morning sun crept slowly across the empty bed as Hunter woke. He vaguely recalled Frank getting dressed and leaving before the sun rose. He thought Frank might have mumbled something about whispering at the stars, but Hunter couldn't remember if it was a dream. It didn't matter, though. The way Frank made love… The way he touched him and made his cock throb with just a whisper…

He sighed just thinking about it. If last night were an example of what being with a male prostitute was like, Hunter needed more. Much more.

He pushed the blanket off and unfurled himself in the warmth of the sun. The sheets held a slight stiffness from their sweaty sex. He inhaled the casual aroma of their musk as the sun reheated it and he wished for more than just the scent of their raw intimacy.

He tucked his hands behind his head and chuckled, recalling the night. He'd wanted Frank street-raw and thought Frank had sensed that. But he'd insisted on a shower anyway. Maybe Frank felt the rough edges had to be smoothed on their first tryst. Or perhaps making Hunter wait, making him taste the scent of his own soap was Frank's way of exacting revenge on the fact that Hunter's blindness had curtailed his usual seductive and exhibitionistic tendencies.

One last good stretch and Hunter rolled his feet to the floor and sat up. "Damn," he said out loud. If he smoked, he'd be desperate for a cigarette right about now. He scratched himself and another smile blossomed.

Frank had spoken of a deep green melancholy on their way back to his apartment and, after last night, Hunter finally understood what he meant.

The answer was in Frank's hands. All of it, right there in the slender wrinkles of his hands – the desperate resilience; the annoyed flamboyance; his personable passivity and his phobic aggressiveness. They were all trapped in the clever lines of his fingers, the hard, unsociable cast of his knuckles, the safe hopelessness of the pads. Sightlings never understood how much you could tell about a person by their hands. Now green melancholy would forever have an association for Hunter, and it wouldn't have anything to do with sadness.

Frank's touch had made Hunter quiver. It made him envious, yet despairing, as if brutality had touched Frank somewhere in his past and left behind a conscious reaction to its potential. And of course, this odd sensation had only made Hunter's desire to explore Frank's body stronger.

He found Frank's wrists thin, almost timid. His nipples were sensitive and extroverted like his belly button – a gregarious, fun-loving bit of flesh whose purpose on Frank seemed wholly deceitful. Frank's legs seemed disbelieving of the entire charade and his feet were down-right pissed off, heckling at Hunter's hands as they passed.

When Hunter ran his fingers through Frank's hair, he found it still damp from the shower. It felt heavy and longish even though it was clipped close on the sides. His ears were energetic and elliptical, resonating with some harsh judgment of youth that had warped them from their previously gullible stature. He was thick-lipped and pouty with long, sharp incisors which gave him the feel of a leer when he grinned.

But to the last, Frank's limbs all bowed to the dictatorial assertiveness of his cock, and that was why Hunter growled and spat like an animal when Frank fucked him to a near senseless abandon.

He sighed and inhaled Frank's aroma one final time. But before he could get up and wash it off, the phone rang. He knew it could only be one person. Very few people had his private number. All business calls went through Margie.

"Sorry," Margie said when he picked up the phone.

Hunter closed his eyes. He'd completely forgotten about their argument. Frank's lovemaking had ensured that. "If you're just calling to make sure I got home okay, it's a little late for that," Hunter told her.

"That too," Margie answered, unperturbed by the jibe.

Hunter was silent for a moment. This was where he was supposed to apologize. But he'd fought long and hard to escape his mother, and harder still to make it on his own. He wasn't about to let anyone, even his closest friend, make him feel guilty because of it.

He took a breath, maybe he was over-reacting. He was a little sensitive about the subject. "Well, I'm actually not sorry," Hunter informed her. "I had an excellent night."

"You did? With who?" Margie demanded immediately. There was a sharp surprise to her voice that almost made him laugh.

"I met him on the way home," Hunter explained.

"Please don't tell me you picked up some disgusting cab driver. That would be so…Eww," Margie said, a shudder of disgust in her voice. They'd commented often enough about the unique individuals who drove the city cabs that it had become a small joke between them.

"I walked home from where you dropped me off."

"All the way? Are you fucking crazy? Anything could have happened!" Margie barked.

"It did happen," Hunter said quietly. He could feel her compulsive curiosity creep down the line and with it a hint of cautious agitation. She knew how large and dangerous his determination to be independent could be. Sometimes, like last night, it bordered on insanity.

"Well, tell me," she said after a long pause. "If it was such a fantastic night and you're still alive, it couldn't have been all bad," she offered, trying to keep the stilted tension of her voice as disinterested as possible.

"I picked up a male prostitute." He pulled the phone away from his ear before she could start screaming, which she did, instantly. She had precise and loud comments about his stupidity, the obviousness of how she'd have felt if anything happened to him, and the suicidal caper his mother would embark upon to get him back under her control when she found out.

"And who's going to tell her?" Hunter asked as he brought the phone back to his ear.

Margie got defensive immediately. Hunter let her verbally backtrack until her concern turned into the self-righteousness she thought she was somehow entitled to being his sighted friend.

"It's over and I'm all right, so will you just shut the fuck up and let me enjoy the after-glow?" Hunter finally spat. Sometimes, she was as bad as his mother.

Margie went mute immediately. They were both pretty lonely, so despite the utter stupidity of dragging a complete stranger back to his apartment, Hunter knew she was well aware of what loneliness was like. For all the bitching, she meant well.

"Thank you," he said. "Now what's up for today?"

Contrite professionalism filled her voice almost immediately, subtly telling him that they hadn't had their last conversation about this particular dalliance. He shook his head and ran his fingers through his hair. He loved her to death, but at times she was too much to bear.

"Noumenon," Margie told him. "The writer is some guy named Francisco. Sax is his agent."

"Christ," Hunter grumbled.

"I thought you'd be happy about that."

"Where are we meeting?"

"The Rat Hole," she answered, knowing he wouldn't allow anyplace else.

"I'll be there at eleven." He hung up, yawned and stretched before making his way to the shower.

Hunter's business was books, audio books to be precise. Not the top shelf bookstore type of books, but the small press, cult following kind. In the business, he was known as 'The Ear' for his ability to match voice, character setting, and auditory scene. His product wasn't anything like those lame author-sits-and reads-into-the-microphone audios people listened to. These were full-scale productions. Some people called them retro, like the old radio programs, but he called them money. He only published on CD and only sold to private booksellers, primarily near college campuses where his following was strongest. He was aware that the kids were converting the CDs to other mediums and putting them on torrent sites and that was fine with him because it grew his audience faster than he ever could alone. But he also had signed collections of everything he produced and every writer that was on his label. And those CDs were a hot ticket, big money collector's items and worth more every time one of those kids downloaded his work. And he was the only dealer for that stuff.

He wasn't rich, and some months he wasn't even comfortable, but the business was his. If people were looking for A River Runs through It, Cold Mountain, or The Color Purple they weren't shopping his product. He looked for something more dangerous, something that cut to the quick in a quickness. He wanted to build smiles one minute, and a blister of desolation in the next. If it wasn't concise and penetrating with an offbeat flavor, then he wasn't interested, nor was his growing fan base.

But lately, he'd been having trouble finding that kind of writing and that was the only reason he was dealing with Sax. Sometimes, Saxby came across an obscure author who had tried all other publishing houses and were now down to Hunter's level. But most of the time, Sax just talked the bullshit monotony his clients wrote and got unceremoniously booted to the door. Hopefully, today would be different.

***

The Rat Hole was just what it sounded like, a sore spot of neglected furniture, contemptible servers, and surly food and drink. Hunter loved the scheming fracas that surrounded its atmosphere, from the ripe odors of the bathrooms, the tepid smell of the staff, and the inhibited aroma of the kitchen.

In its heyday, if there had ever been one, the place was supposedly themed on Cagney's infamous but unuttered line about dirty rats. Judging from Margie's verbal description of the place, it was a major neurosis of the original decorator who had plastered the walls with yellowed photos of old time gangsters and movie stars. Apparently the concept had never taken, but that hadn't stopped the restaurant from devolving down to its rightful name.

Hunter walked in to his usual warm welcome.

"You gonna take my table all fucking day, Batman?" the waitress asked when the door closed behind him.

"Got to make a living, Connie," Hunter replied. She was an immense black woman over six feet tall, and from the trays she hauled around the place, Hunter guessed she had arms like a linebacker. He'd asked Margie to describe her once and all she could say was scary.

"Yeah, me too, you know?" Connie bit back at him.

"Margie here yet?" Hunter asked.

"She's there. You need some help?"

He turned to give Connie a faux stare. This was also part of their ritual.

"Piss on you, then," Connie said, turning away from him.

And that's what kept Hunter coming back. There was no sympathy for anybody. People from the lowest dregs of society came here – some of them even died here – and they all got the same got-my-own-fucking-problems deference that everyone else did, regardless of their social malady. He loved it.

"Why do we have to meet everyone in this shithole?" Margie asked once again.

Hunter found his chair and sat. "Don't bullshit me, Margie. The place is growing on you." He smiled. "I can tell."

"Yeah, like mold, but that doesn't answer my question."

"It keeps people from getting their expectations up," Hunter explained.

"There isn't any place from here but up," she protested.

"Exactly."

Margie and Hunter had worked together since he'd moved to Atlanta and jumped on the idea of specialized audio books. She'd explained her appearance as fat, frumpy, and fervently futile, but in her voice Hunter found passion, vague dignity, and a wily intellect rendered sharp from an unvoiced cruelty in her past.

She was a person upon whom threats and torments only lubricated and released glacial ruthlessness, which she usually tried to keep hidden. Hunter had pulled that unattractive beast from her depths only once. But it had made him realize that, behind her persistent quarrelsomeness, they were the best of friends, even if they did irk the shit out of each other.

After they ordered, ate, and tossed a few more insults back and forth with Connie, a blubbery inhalation of breath from behind Hunter announced that Saxby had arrived.

"Are you going to stand there all day?" Hunter asked without turning around.

Chairs scraped on either side of him. From his left, Hunter got the odor of cheap cigars and week-old sweat. That would be Sax; his nicotine-laden breath was so heavy it fell to the table like a stone every time Hunter met him. On the right, the odor was predominantly greasy smoke, as if from a deeper dining pit than the one they were in now.

"You brought me a fry cook?" Hunter asked Sax.

"Man, get off my nuts, Hunter. I brought him to you because he's eclectic enough that the big boys won't touch him. What he does to survive is his own business," Saxby answered with a snarl.

True, Hunter conceded with a silent nod. He swung his unfunctioning gaze to the author. It was one of the first times Sax had ever given him a straight answer. It made him wonder if Sax was finally starting to figure out that the bullshit he flung to other publishing houses wasn't going to work when he brought potential clients to him. Hunter knew what he wanted from his authors, but Saxby had yet to figure it out. Maybe this was a start.

"Where do you work?" Hunter asked the author, Francisco.

"The Pit."

Hunter nodded. "Good barbecue. You the fry man?"

"Yeah, how'd you know?"

Francisco was nervous, but curious too. His voice sounded a little like the sound of scrabbled dirt; not quite gravel and not quite loam. It was as if he made soft chipping sounds when he spoke – a light rustling vocalization that got its point across but sounded perpetually unsure of itself.

But that could have been the meeting too. Hunter had no doubt that all his previous rejection slips had been simple form letters saying thanks, but no fucking way, much like the correspondence received by most of Saxby's other clients.

"I have a very acute sense of smell," Hunter answered his question. "Now tell me how you came to me."

"Saxby," Francisco said simply.

Hunter heard him take a drink from one of the glasses on the table. Margie would've undoubtedly snapped his head from his shoulders had Hunter not been there, but he was starting to like this guy. He was unpretentious, to the point, and didn't offer bullshit when a simple yes or no would do. For a brief moment, Hunter had to wonder how he'd ever gotten involved with Saxby.

"What else did Sax tell you about me?" Hunter asked.

"He said you were blind and a pain in the ass, but that you got results when you put someone under contract. He also told me a couple of your authors have gone on to bigger things because of the work they did with you."

Margie was silent, as was Sax. They both knew Hunter's next question. "You know I'm not going to make you a millionaire, right?"

Francisco laughed. "I just like to write. If I can make a few bucks off it, I'm happy; if it goes beyond that, great. I don't have any delusions."

"So why not a vanity publisher?" Hunter asked.

"Well, that's kind of dated. And I'm a fry cook. I don't have the money for that type of gig. The only reason I'm here is because a few friends said I should publish. Then, when I mentioned that Sax mentioned you, they said that was even better. I had them pull out some of your stuff and...I dug it. And here I am." He shrugged.

"And these friends... Were they your friends or people in the book business?" Hunter asked.

"Just friends."

Fans, Hunter rephrased it in his head. Fans who were already aware of Hunter's label and would be an immediate street team for Francisco. "And if I told you that you had to rewrite the whole manuscript?" Hunter inquired. It would never happen because Margie vetted virtually everything before it came to him, but it was nice to get a feel for how willing an author was to accept his input.

"That would suck," Francisco answered honestly.

"Good, thanks for coming," Hunter said.

"That's it?"

"That's it, for now. I haven't heard your story yet. You passed Margie," Hunter said with a jut of his chin across the table, "but not me. After I hear it, I'll call Sax and he'll call you."

Francisco seemed to think about it for a moment. "Okay."

Hunter turned to Sax. "Saxby, get some goddamn decent cigars, will you? That shit you're smoking is killing me, and probably everyone else in here."

"Yeah? So make me a fucking millionaire. I'll smoke whatever you want, including your dick. Margie," he said with a nod as they got up.

"That man is so disgusting," Margie said.

"I think he has the hots for you," Hunter told her after the bell on the door rang their exit.

"That's even more disgusting," Margie retorted. "He's so fucking gross," she added with a shudder. "Besides, he wants to smoke your wood, not mine."

"So tell me about this manuscript," Hunter said after they had a laugh. What he heard was weak, but it had possibilities. Their last big run had come from a guy who was a professional sign holder. He stood outside businesses with signs like "We buy gold!" and "Mattresses start at $200!" and dictated an entire manuscript into a mini recorder. Most of his employers thought he was a crackhead or an ex-con, but he was pulling down royalties from the worldwide cult following Hunter had built for him. He'd quit the sign business for a while and then went back to it when he realized it provided him with the mental space he needed to create. His streetwise muse, he'd called it. Hunter didn't care what he called it, just that it worked.

"You're already hooked," Margie said about Francisco's manuscript. "I knew you would be. The Coalition will have seizures."

Hunter smiled, delighted by the idea, his mind whirling with attributes for the voices. "And you know what that means?"

"Free advertising," Margie replied in a drone. She hated the marketing side of things, but it was a significant part of her job.

"I'm assuming there's more," Hunter said as he reached for his coffee.

"It needs a lot of work. But the bones are there. If we can hit the spot with the voices and the marketing, this could develop a real following... A new one with broader revenue streams," she advised.

Hunter tossed the idea around for a moment. She was right. "Okay, contract it up and put the float out for a voice call, nonstandard. I want some fresh sounds. And I want to go through the manuscript more. Can you email me the file?" Hunter asked.

"Already done," she said. "It will be waiting for you when you get home."

He heard her pen skittering across the paper as she took notes. With all the electronic gadgets she had, Hunter had once asked why she took notes on paper. She told him that thieves were less likely to steal a small notepad than they were an electronic gizmo. The notepad didn't break. It didn't lose information and she liked the idea of having a pen around to jab some dickhead in the face if he made the dire error of thinking she was an easy target. It was a hope that never seemed to come true.

For his part, Hunter hated toting an electronic note taker around. It wasn't often that he needed anything written down. He had excellent recall.

"Right, now tell me about last night," Margie said with a crisp bit of efficiency.

"I thought we discussed this," Hunter answered cooly.

"It's like this," Margie growled as she slapped her pen on the table. "I went home last night pissed and upset, figuring you'd be doing the same. But nooo, you're getting your brains fucked out and I'm stuck at home with my dildo. Now stop screwing around and tell me."

Hunter picked up his coffee cup, turned as if looking around the restaurant, and said, "I don't know what you're talking about."

"Hunter!"

He lowered his voice and leaned toward her. "It was great."

"Weren't you scared?"

"Shitless, but I think that's what made it so good."

Margie put her elbows on the table and proper her chin in her hands. "What was he like?" She wanted all the details. She liked a good man sex story and they both knew it. They'd talked about doing audio man-on-man fiction at one time but finally realized that neither of them would be able to create a complete CD without running home to masturbate every hour or two.

Hunter had to really think about her question before he could answer. It was hard to put the tactile sensations a blind person felt into words a seeing person could understand. Like, how could he explain green melancholy without her getting caught up in a Webster's definition?

Frank was amazing last night, and not just in a sexual way. But as Hunter began to divulge all their horny escapades, he changed his mind about telling her and closed his mouth. "I think I'll keep it to myself."

"Huh?" she asked in disbelief. Her exasperation was almost a physical thing. She was all but vibrating with the anticipation. She'd given Hunter the scene play-by-play as it happened on her last date and she wanted the same.

"Private, Margie," he told her.

"Fuck. Okay, how much?"

He mumbled a response that was vague enough to mean absolutely nothing.

"What?" Margie asked, her neck coming forward as if she hadn't heard him quite right.

Hunter cleared his throat "Two-fifty."

"For a piece of ass?" she blurted across the restaurant.

Hunter felt his face flush even though he couldn't see all the heads suddenly turned toward them. The unexpected lull in conversation told him enough. "A little louder, Margie, maybe you can stop traffic next time."

"Two hundred and fifty bucks," she hissed. "Christ."

"That's actually a good bit less than a decent agency would charge," Hunter informed her.

"What?! You can buy a crack whore for twenty bucks."

"A crack whore? Really? What about my safety? Isn't that what you were bitching about yesterday?" he demanded, his tone an accusation in itself. "You're worried about the cost of a professional escort, so I should save a few bucks and pick up some methed-out street whore for the price of a rock? That doesn't make a bit of sense."

"It's not about the money…" Margie countered quickly. "You know what I mean."

They were silent for a moment, on the edge of repeating the same argument they'd had the day before.

"I never booked one," Hunter offered, trying to keep the peace. "I just checked on the price. You know? A little rent-a-dick once in a while never hurt anyone. You should try it. And last night, he was worth every single penny."

"You're insane, you know that?" Margie said, tight-lipped. "Your mother would have a fucking aneurysm."

Hunter smiled at that thought. "I know."

"All right, stop your damned gloating," Margie grunted. "And don't expect me to tell you shit about my next date."

"It wasn't a date," Hunter corrected her. "It was…a rendezvous. And it just sort of happened. I'll tell you what, if I had the money, I'd do him again tonight. Fuck, I'd do him right now."

"That good, for real?" Margie asked, her interest rekindled.

"It was..." he shrugged, "different from what I expected, and hot, really fucking hot."

Margie suddenly got quiet; like she did when she started moving into what Hunter called her Lydia mode – the over-protective friend cautioning him like a parent.

"Don't do it," Hunter warned.

"What?"

The false innocence in her voice told him he was exactly on point. "Don't lecture me."

He didn't understand why she was so pushy about his safety lately. If he were a sightling, her attitude concerning his independence would never enter into their friendship. But because he was blind, sightlings took it as their privilege to treat him as a weak inferior because they thought he didn't understand how vulnerable he was. It was that very presumption which had driven him from his mother's house. "Just don't, Margie."

Margie fell silent again and backed off, but they both knew she wanted to give him a lecture. "Okay, whatever. So shoot me if I worry about you," Margie grumbled as she shuffled some papers around and shifted their focus to business. "I called Red yesterday about..."

Hunter tuned her out immediately. He was resentful that she had, once again, been so ready to launch into another speech about how he needed to be cautious because of his blindness.

He knew the risks involved. He'd always known the risks;

his mother had never, ever let him forget them. When would people realize he was capable of running his own damned life?

He blew out a frustrated breath as his mind wandered back to last night. The recall changed his attitude immediately and he smiled to himself. The fanciful notion of meeting up with Frank again tickled his thoughts with all the sinful erotic things they hadn't gotten to in their one night together. There was no denying Frank thrilled him. The sex was fantastic. The fact that Frank was a prostitute excited Hunter beyond anything logical. Frank knew how to make love, and better, he knew how to fuck like a carnal beast. Hell, his ass was still sore. He chuckled.

"What?" Margie asked, her diatribe interrupted.

Hunter waved it off. "Nothing. Go on. I'm listening." But he wasn't. And if only because he realized that the best part of the entire evening was the fact that Frank made him feel like a whole and complete man. He didn't treat him like other men had. Frank was like the last sarcastic tingle of a lethal dose of arsenic and Hunter wanted every dark and erotic swallow, despite the risk. Maybe in spite of it.

He ran his hand absentmindedly through his hair as Margie blathered. He was completely lost in the fantasy he'd conjured up as he climbed into the shower this morning.

***

Frank rented a room in a derelict hotel in the most rundown part of the city. Outside, the disheveled remnants of humanity camped in doorways while religious lunatics screamed on the street corners about the second coming. Inside, it was a place of hunger. It carried the smell of age and faded paint with an underlying aroma of damp rot.

"You like it, don't you?" Frank questioned him.

He'd figured out Hunter's secret. Hunter could hear it in his voice.

Frank stepped up next to him. "You're the kind my mama warned me about," Frank whispered in his ear. "Dirty boy," he'd added, like it was an accusation.

Hunter chewed on his lower lip. He'd never told anyone. Not a soul. Even now, he couldn't bring the word to his lips. But the twang of Frank's voice made his cock hard with desire. It overrode his senses. "Yes." He couldn't deny it. He wanted to fuck like animals with the sweat and the heat from their bodies laying another pungent wreath on the carpet beneath his knees.

But Frank had other ideas. There was the whisper of the shirt going over his head, the earthy aroma of his armpits, and the speechless clatter of his shoes hitting the floor before Hunter was even allowed to move.

Frank cleared his throat of cigarettes and drew Hunter to his feet. He kissed Hunter hard. The prickly rasp of his morning whiskers scratched against Hunter's jaw as their lips ground together. He took Hunter's hands and put them on his ass so Hunter could feel the leather pants he'd worn. Pants that were rude with the trapped scent of his sweaty, semi-hard cock.

Hunter groaned.

Frank stuck his hand inside the leather, stroked his cock a few times and then put his fingers under Hunter's nose, letting him get the musk of a man heated with desire. "You can have it, if you can take my pants off," Frank taunted.

But Hunter couldn't get them off. He could feel the thick veins of Frank's cock through the leather, caress the length of it, gnaw at the bulge, but he could not undo the fucking knots that held Frank's pants closed.

Hunter didn't have to see Frank to see his smile. The hitch of his breath as he struggled and rubbed against him told Hunter everything.

Frank took his wrists, spun him and pressed his face into the damp, ripe sheets. He filled Hunter's nostrils with the odors of sex and arousal, with the tingling fragrances of fear and lust. He made Hunter smell all those he'd conquered before Hunter's arrival.

"You want this cock?" Frank demanded as he rubbed it against Hunter's ass. "Do you?"

"Yes," Hunter gasped. He knew that in the midst of this diseased abode, Frank would tie him to the bed and stand over him, disconcerting, immoral, and yet utterly beautiful – a stark reminder of the beauty of Lucifer and the subtle taint of his hallucinatory deviousness. And there among the barren forgetfulness of that room they'd fuck, and fuck hard.

***

Hunter had almost come. Almost. But the self-deceit of his fantasy vanished with the last of the hot water and the certainty that

Frank could afford something above a dungeon-like rented room and dirty, thrift shop sheets.

Still, Hunter mused as he recalled it again. Maybe if he could afford it, he'd ask Frank to wander barefoot and bring the taste of the city back to his apartment – the smoky, dusty, urine stench of it mixed in with Frank's own vinegary flavor. Blend in the rough odor of the cigarettes he smoked and....hmm.

So kinky, he heard Frank whisper.

If he only knew.

Hunter understood that most people would find his fantasies vulgar, maybe even disgusting. But a sightling could never comprehend how erotic all the other senses were. They thought a blindfold could help them match his arousal. Not so. He went by taste and touch and smell every day just to survive. He could feel how a man's cock throbbed and quivered just before it exploded inside of him. He could differentiate the salt flavoring his skin. He could smell the level of his partner's arousal as if it were a taste.

Sightlings didn't know these things. They couldn't. They were too wrapped up in visual cues to understand how far eroticism and beauty went beyond mere sight.

He took a deep breath, thinking about Frank again. Maybe they could get some claustrophobic little room somewhere and fuck like feral cats rutting in an alley...

But no, that wasn't Frank. He wasn't cats in an alley. Frank was a big cat on the African plain – hard, muscular, grunting with each forceful thrust; calves thick and beefy – a lion in heat conquering his queen.

And Jesus holy mother, he had a cock on him…

"...so it'll be Monday then?" Margie asked. "You there?" She waved her hand in Hunter's face. She knew how much he hated it and how fast it would get his attention.

"Yes, Monday. The sound lab is booked?" Hunter asked, silently adjusting himself beneath the table.

"Nine o'clock."

"Okay, I'll see you then."

Margie hesitated. She so wanted to give him advice about Frank, as if it were something more than a one-night stand.

But Hunter wasn't naive. The fantasy was nice, but the reality he lived in wouldn't allow Frank to become anything regular, even if he could afford it. "Go home, Margie. I'll see you Monday. This is the weekend I have to deal with my mother."

She reluctantly pulled her backpack from under the table and shuffled her way out in silence.

Hunter knew she was gone when Connie came up beside him. "Can I have my table back now, Batman? Or, are you gonna be groping around here for a few more hours fucking up my tips?"

Hunter smiled. He loved the raw abrasiveness of this woman. "What would I do without you, Connie?"

"You'd still be sucking your momma's titties. Now git somewhere. I got bills to pay and the old man ain't worth shit."

"Then why do you stay with him?" Hunter asked.

"'Cause he can fuck like a rabbit when he's sober, that's

why. Now git! Why do I stay? Damn kids ain't got no manners these days. Asking me a question such as that..." Connie grumbled as she walked away.

She kept mumbling as Hunter left, half serious, half joking, but beneath that brusque nature and ribald tongue was a heart of gold.

***

Hunter had literally stumbled into this uncompromising eatery called the Rat Hole as a stranger who had finally escaped Lydia's clawing grasp. From his earliest beginnings, he'd lived sheltered and unmolested, knowing only the thick trees of his mother's yard and the hard scrabble of an asphalt road that hemmed him in like a river. At the Rat Hole, he'd lost his societal virginity.

"You gonna nurse that goddamned cup all day or what?" Connie had barked at Hunter that first time.

"I'd like to eat," Hunter told her.

"So eat. Shit ain't gonna come floating outta the kitchen. You tell me what you want. I tell the asshole in the back, and once the grease is hot enough to kill off most of the germs, I bring it out. That's how it works around here, wonder boy."

"I can't read the menu," Hunter had told her, expecting a monumental change in demeanor.

"And that means what? You're retarded, or blind, or both?"

"Blind," Hunter answered.

"Sheeeee-ut," Connie said as she snatched the menu from somewhere off the table and read the entrees like a clerk of the court reading a list of previous convictions. "Now what the fuck you want, Batman? I got other tables."

Hunter smiled to keep from laughing out loud. He loved her. "What's your name?"

"You gonna report me to the manager? I'll save you the trouble. Larry!" She bellowed across the restaurant and above the racket of the kitchen. "Larry, got Batman here wanna complain about the quality of the service!"

She turned back to Hunter, probably expecting him to get up and leave. He could hear the smoky rasp of her inhalation, no doubt from the strain the shouting had caused her.

"Actually, I was going to ask for you by name the next time I came in," Hunter said.

"Christ, why do I always get 'em?" She didn't believe a word of it. "What do you want then, Batman?"

He ordered a burger and fries. When he was done, he put the exact change for the check on the table and left a twenty for a tip under the plate. Mostly so nobody would steal it, but also to make sure she understood that it was no mistake. The next time he came in she had the same attitude, but the food was in clock positions around the plate, so he knew they'd hit it off.

Hunter never told her, but she was the very first person he'd met outside of the school for the blind who didn't feel sorry for him. The strength he gained from that one contact was worth more twenties than he could pile on all the tables she served. Everybody else he knew hated her attitude, and this restaurant; but to Hunter, she was a lozenge for all the unwanted pity he'd had shit on him every day previous to that.

Chapter 4

Life in Lydia's house seemed, from the time Hunter was old enough to realize it, as if he were perpetually drowning. And if not in his mother's maternal waters, then there always lingered the threat of him possibly being thrown overboard for mutinous behavior. Lydia told him the world was a place that he didn't want to be in. It ate his kind up in an instant, not even bothering to wipe the blood from its lips before looking for another snack.

He had only to wander outdoors barefoot, feel the stir of life growing between his toes, smell the nurturing air of alfalfa, and touch the sharp, razored edge of existence before death was thrust up behind it.

"Smell the loam," Lydia had said, grasping a handful under his nose. "That's the smell of death."

But Hunter found life in the aroma. He found regurgitation and the stubborn ache of an eternal spiral that left panic on those near its end. He smelled flowers bending in slow ruin, seeds hard and bold with new life, a river moving lazy through shallow greens. There was affection in that dirt – a touch of flesh meeting the crumbled hand of God. It was the opposite of how his mother felt about everything.

Lydia lived outside of Atlanta in a small town of squares, old oaks, and Spanish moss. Hunter made the trip back to her house about once a month, all the voices and smells on the journey becoming as familiar to him as his own apartment. The only thing that changed was the company on the bus. With each trip, Hunter learned a little more about the travesty of the human condition, something his mother still thought she could protect him from.

He sat in the front of the bus across from the driver so Bob wouldn't feel obliged to come traipsing down the aisle to inform him of his stop. Bob smelled like he bathed in Old Spice but never actually had any water touch his body. And the seat Bob sat on emitted a noxious odor of stuck-on shit each time he adjusted himself, which was often. Had it not been for his genuine kindness, Hunter would've saved his senses the assault and moved to the rear of the bus.

As it was, Bob made sure Hunter was safe and comfortable just before they left each stop. "Ready?" he'd ask after each one.

"Ready," Hunter would answer, the blind simpleton he thought Bob imagined him.

"Busy trip," Hunter said, noting the menagerie of odors that came with the entrance of each group. Vicks VapoRub, car grease, Kool-Aid, licorice, grape chewing gum, sweat, leather, hair oil, more sweat, oranges, the curdle of sour breast milk, urine, Icy Hot, and a whole other host of industrialized miasma he couldn't even name. This was why sightlings never understood the sense of smell. They covered it up or ignored it.

Hunter smiled when people came aboard because he could hear Bob make unconscious noises and grunts as he evaluated his fares. The regulars, like Hunter, were greeted with a friendly word and a question about some family member. The ladies, both younger and older, got a cordial 'ma'am' and help with bags or small children. Blacks and Latinos got a miniscule click of his teeth as if shearing away at a prejudice Bob would claim he had no hold to.

"Holidays coming," Bob replied as they pulled away from the smell of diesel and French fries outside. "Money's tight, people moving about to get settled or start fresh or visit those they'd rather not see when St. Nick pokes around. It gets like this every year about this time. You get a lot of kids on the circuit too, heading further south or west for warmer climates."

"The circuit?" Hunter asked.

"Runaways and deadbeats going from city to city, living in abandoned houses and getting drugs and food any way they can. Got some special name for themselves, but in my book they're just the youngest generation of bums looking for handouts from the taxpayers. I got a grandson out in California calls his momma about once a month for money which, of course, she sends. Kid's got a brain, but absolutely no desire to use it while he's getting a free ride."

"What's his mother say about this? If you don't mind my asking," Hunter said, in awe of the freedom such an endeavor would've brought when he was younger.

"Said he's feeling his oats, if you can believe that one," Bob replied. "I say crack him upside his head, cut his hair, and lock him in his room until he comes to his senses. But then, I'm just a bus driver, what do I know?"

"A bit more than his mother, I'd say." Hunter lied to make the rides to his mother's at least tolerable. He could hear Bob grunt and smile in agreement. But he knew that, like Lydia, Bob would've kept him locked away for safety's sake, much as Lydia had tried to do when he was a kid.

***

Hunter was seven, wrapped in the stifling familiarity of his mother's home. He was sick and feverish, but could clearly hear tires crunching through the snow toward their house. The noise was like a premonition that his life was about to change. He crawled from his bed with a blanket wrapped around him as the sound grew louder.

He went to the door, listening as a car pulled in and stopped. Two doors opened and four feet shuffled through the snow. He heard his mother bump against an end table in the living room as she pushed the curtain aside to see who their visitors were. He knew she was surprised to see him out of bed when she rounded the corner because she hesitated slightly as he reached for the doorknob.

"Wait." It was almost a whisper, as if she'd had the same premonition and had thought about not answering. But the door was already swinging open.

"You must be Hunter," said an unfamiliar but warmth-filled voice. "Is your mom...? Oh, Mrs. Stephens, I'm Ellie Richfield. We've come to talk to you about getting Hunter into school."

"School?" Lydia had asked as she moved forward and took a protective hold of the door.

"Yes, Mrs. Stephens. The law requires...."

"My son is blind, Miss Richfield. The local school has no accommodations for his disability. I did check," Lydia informed her.

"Yes, ma'am, that's true, but there are schools specifically set up for the blind and Hunter is old enough that he should be attending one already."

Hunter heard strength and determination in her voice, and he'd no doubt Lydia heard it too though she probably perceived it as a challenge or a potential confrontation.

"Just who are you with, Ms. Richfield? I don't have the money to send him to a private school, and he is doing quite well despite that."

Hunter heard Ms. Richfield snap a card out from somewhere and hand it to his mother. "I'm with Social Services, Mrs. Stephens, and we're here to help you find a place for Hunter. If we could come in, we could show you how it wouldn't cost you a thing, and it would still be a great school."

"And if not?" Lydia asked.

The question hung like flypaper swirling in the air, all the dead carcasses a tribute to that particular twist of life called consequences, which, in this case, remained unspoken. Hunter didn't understand what the word meant at that time, but he grew a great appreciation for it later.

"Come in," Lydia ordered with resignation. And that began Hunter's eventual emancipation, but not Lydia's persistent attempts at subverting it.

***

"Your stop, Hunter," Bob said from his perch.

Hunter got up, smelling the oily odor of Garret's Garage outside. He thanked Bob and felt his chest constrict as he stepped down the stairs toward home. Not his home anymore, he corrected himself, Lydia's.

He moved a few paces away from the bus and let it drive off and leave him in a cloud of exhaust. He stood for a moment to orient himself by the sounds echoing from the garage.

Garret had be-bop blaring and Hunter chuckled because all of Garret's customers claimed a loathing. Yet through the years, Hunter had invariably heard many, if not most of them, humming to one of the latest top ten, sometimes shocking themselves with a verbal scowl when Hunter pointed it out.

Garret was in his late sixties and claimed his radio dial flipped over a broad spectrum to keep him young. That, with the fact that his son Toby couldn't get enough of the music, meant that the situation was unlikely to change.

"Boy, what are you doing standing out there? Come on in," Garret shouted through the door and over the radio. "Expect you need a lift. Coke first?" Garret asked as Hunter came in. "Like the tunes?" he asked as he turned them down to a conversational level.

"Always," Hunter answered.

"How you been?"

"I've been well, Garret. How's Toby?"

Hunter noted that the smile in Garret's voice faded almost immediately. "Not so good today. Had him a scare a few weeks back and hurt himself. He'll be right as rain soon enough."

His tone of voice said just the opposite, but Hunter let it go. Garret was a private man and when it came to Toby, his Down's syndrome son, he bordered on clandestine.

"He'll sure be upset he missed you, though," Garret added.

"Could we swing by your place first?" Hunter asked. "I'd like to see him too."

Gratefulness and sincerity radiated from Garret like a wave of heat. "Sure! Let me close up and we'll hop to it."

He went to close the bay doors while Hunter finished off the Coke by the counter. From the echo of the door's rumbling, he guessed the place to be almost empty – most of Garret's regulars having died off or gone to speedier operations.

Growing up, he'd spent many days behind the counter babysitting the place while Garret ran off on a quick tow job. Garret always had a cheerful word and never pitied the fact that he'd lost his wife during childbirth, or that Toby had been born with Down's. A few of Hunter's friends from the blind school said Garret probably liked Hunter so much because he wished his own son had been born blind instead of with Down's. But Hunter thought that a cruel assessment of a man they never met. He never heard such a sentiment in Garret's words. Garret loved Toby without reserve.

They left the garage shortly after Garret closed up. But when Garret pulled over prematurely, Hunter tensed. He could smell the thick scent of horses and knew they weren't anywhere near Garret's house yet. By his estimation, they were still a few miles away.

"We're here already?" he asked, feigning ignorance.

"No," Garret answered. "I... Well, Toby's bound to say something so I may as well tell you first." He drew a breath before he continued. "A couple of boys came over from Pooler and put a scare into Toby while I was out on a tow job. They roughed him up a bit too. I was out picking up Bill Mixby's car...." He trailed off leaving his guilt sitting on the seat between them.

"They broke his wrist, Hunter; broke that poor baby's wrist because I didn't have twenty bucks in the till." His voice was choked with anger and undiluted sorrow. "They robbed him because he has Down's and they thought they could get away with it." He took another deep breath to calm himself. "Anyway, he might mention it. He'll probably ask you to sign his cast. It's supposed to come off next Tuesday, but I'm sure he'd be tickled if you did."

"Did they get away with it?" Hunter asked.

Garret started the truck again and pulled into the road before he answered. "No. Drew Thompson's an old friend of mine. He knew Toby's mama. He's the warden out at the county jail and checked on them for me. Seems three little white boys have taken to shaving their legs and using M&Ms for eyeshadow these days. Gonna get themselves a mandatory ten years in the state pen for armed robbery is what he said. I guess it ain't so funny now that they're the ones getting fucked with. 'Scuse my French," he added.

He paused for a moment. "Anyway, I didn't think Lydia told you about it and I just wanted to warn you before we got there."

Lydia hadn't said anything and Hunter knew it was likely

that she wouldn't. Toby had been as much an anathema as he was. "Is he afraid to go back to the garage, or is it you?" Hunter asked.

Garret weighed Hunter's question before he answered. "He's having nightmares still, but I suppose it's me more than him. Sometimes I forget and treat him older than his mind is."

"You couldn't have known, Garret. And he's been running those pumps alone for years."

"Yeah, well, the world's changed since then," Garret answered sharply. "It about broke my heart finding him like that, Hunter. There's just the two of us in this world and if I can't look out for him on my own property, how much use am I?"

"Are you thinking about closing up?" Hunter asked, having heard the indecision in his tone.

"Been thinking about it for a while," Garret replied. "His mama would've scalped me, and business just ain't what it used to be. It seems like we're farting around more than getting any actual work done these days."

Hunter was silent for a moment, thinking how close Toby's circumstances were to his own. "Don't coop him up and close off the world just because he met some of its misery, Garret. That garage is the whole world to him. You won't be doing him any favors. No matter what you do, you can't protect him from every pain this planet has to offer."

"He's not like you, Hunter. He can't overcome his disability. All he's ever going to do is love his daddy. That's it," Garret said with some finality.

"Maybe so, but boxing him up in the house isn't going to do anything but relieve your own anxiety and cut him off from everyone else who loves him. And then what does he do when you're gone?" Hunter asked.

"We're here," Garret said as they pulled into the driveway. He was avoiding the question that Hunter already heard weighing on his conscience. The tow truck rumbled to a stop and Hunter heard Toby come bursting out the door, Hunter's name at the very front of his lips.

"Hunter!" he yelled in excitement and jerked the truck door open. As Hunter climbed out, he could hear Toby's feet tapping on the ground like a puppy dancing around in anticipation.

"Bad men hurt me, Hunter," he said as he grabbed Hunter's free hand and shoved it onto his cast.

Toby usually didn't do that. Both Garret and Hunter had taught him early on that it wasn't polite to grab at a blind man, even if you meant to help him. You always had to ask first. His sudden grip made Hunter understand how much the robbery had jarred him and how much it still bothered him. He wondered if Garret was right about closing the place up after all.

"Are you okay? This seems awfully big for you," Hunter asked as he felt along the cast.

"I'm a big boy now. Nurse Parker told me so. See, feel my other arm." He slowly took Hunter's hand and placed it on his good arm. The kid was built like a steelworker, but he wouldn't hurt a fly. And he was no child, not anymore.

Garret came around the truck. "Bravest soul ever to get a cast is what the nurse said," Garret explained, thumping Toby on the back as he drew them toward the house.

Once the cast was signed, new toys were trolleyed out and a few games were played before Garret sent Toby to the kitchen to start their supper.

"You asked me a question earlier," Garret said, "and I've meant to talk to you about it for a while now."

"About when you're gone?" Hunter asked.

"Yeah."

Hunter waited for more, but it didn't seem to be coming. Then he realized what Garret was actually asking. "Garret, I couldn't possibly... I can barely fend for myself."

"Money wouldn't be a problem. Most of Dot's insurance is still left. I never touched it. Plus there'll be mine, the house, and the land if I ain't sold it by then. I need someone I can trust with him, Hunter."

"Me?"

"You're the only one he'd be comfortable with, and the only one I would trust. There ain't no one else. The state would put him in a home somewhere then stick the money in their coffers and spend it on some political bullshit out Atlanta way."

"No one?" Hunter asked.

"All Dot's people died years back, and I been on my own since I was fourteen. Far as I know, I ain't got no kin either – none I know or would trust with Toby."

"You're asking a lot, Garret. And I'm in no position to make a decision like this right now. And the other thing, I'd never come back here to live. Toby would have to come to me. I don't know if he'd adjust to the city." And, of course, there was the fact that Hunter was gay, but that didn't need to be spoken by either of them.

"I know that," Garret said. "Just think about it. I'm not asking for answers now."

They dropped Hunter off an hour later, Toby unusually quiet as they pulled up to Lydia's house near the center of town.

"I tell you she signed his cast?" Garret asked.

"Lydia?"

"Mm, shocked me too. A few months ago she wouldn't touch him with a ten-foot pole, then this. Something's going on."

"Damned right about that," Hunter mumbled as he climbed out.

He knew something was wrong as soon as Garret's truck had pulled out and the coil of Lydia's tongue hadn't yet been snapped in his direction. She usually met Hunter on the doorstep with a hot oral brand for his indiscretion at having Garret drive him over, and, indirectly, for abandoning her loving embrace. Not so today.

"Mom?" Hunter called out when he walked in the door. The house seemed empty and smelled vastly different from its typical antiseptic odor of straight bleach. Ripe fruit, that's what he smelled, and an undercurrent of...alcohol?

"Mom?"

The whispery rasp of her pants announced her entrance into

the room, but she said nothing. She just stood there. She'd stopped doing that when he was about twelve and started demanding his privacy. She'd walked in while he was having a wank and even though she'd gone rushing out, a thought always worried him that she might've been standing there watching him before she freaked out. The idea of it had made him groan with untold embarrassment and he'd locked his door ever since.

"Is something wrong? Are you okay?"

"I'm fine," Lydia answered.

"Are you sure?" Hunter asked after a long silence.

"I'm sure."

Hunter sniffed. "What's that smell?"

"I'm baking."

Hunter turned to her voice in complete astonishment. He made his way to the kitchen and sat down with a thump. He had to sit. Lydia Stephens was baking. Baking! Like she'd morphed into Mrs. Cleaver during his absence.

"It...smells good," he offered because he could think of nothing else to say. "Are you sure you're okay?"

"Quite. And thank you. It's banana bread."

"When did you start baking?"

"There's a lot you don't know about me, Hunter. And, to be honest, I didn't expect you this weekend. I made other plans."

"You didn't expect... Am I in the right house?" he asked, utterly bewildered. "The last time I checked, I'm always home, as required, on the third Saturday of each month. Those were your rules."

"Don't be a jackass," Lydia snapped. "I didn't raise you that way and it doesn't suit you."

Hunter didn't have to see the curl of her lip. He could hear it in her words.

"You've begrudged these weekends since you left. I didn't think once a month would curtail your lifestyle all that much," she added with a small jeer. "You don't call, you don't write, you just pop up in and expect me to drop everything for you. Well, this is to inform you that I'm done worrying about whether your big city antics are going to get you robbed or killed. Is that easy enough for you?"

"You're dying, aren't you?" Hunter asked. The thought of it bothered him much more than he wanted to acknowledge.

She laughed. "No, dearest one, but it's good to see you still care," she said as she came over and tapped on his cheek with a floury hand. "I don't plan on dying anytime soon if I can help it. Now, can I call you a cab to take you back to the bus station?"

"You're...throwing me out?" Hunter stammered.

"Yes, Hunter. Your mommy has other plans today and you're not a part of them. So, what will it be?"

"I...a cab, I guess, yes."

"Good, hang on." She went over and made a series of calls to the bus station and the cab company. "All set," she said when she put the phone down. "They have a bus going back tonight. It leaves around five. The cab will be here in a few minutes, but you'll have a wait at the bus station."

"You'd tell me if you were sick, wouldn't you?"

"Probably," she answered slowly. "The cab will be here shortly, so you may want to wait on the porch."

"The porch? What the hell is going on here?" Hunter demanded. "Do you have a man in the house? Is that it?" Hunter sniffed at the air as if somehow his blindness had given him the super nasal powers of a hound dog as most people supposed. "You all but demand that I make this trip back here once a month or be committed, and now you're tossing me into the street? Maybe there should be a requirement that I call first."

"That's an excellent idea," she answered with a humorous lilt in her voice.

His mouth fell open. This wasn't the woman who raised him. It couldn't even be an alien pod-person replica. Lydia wasn't quite the bitch he portrayed her as when he was in the city, but she was pretty damned close.

Her overprotectiveness had verged on smothering him when he was younger. The rebellion that ensued because of it was what made him run to the sounds and smells of the big city when he was twenty-three. He had to escape before Lydia's fears turned into a cocoon he couldn't escape.

But this... This was not Lydia.

"Cab's here," she announced when the horn honked out front.

***

"Sounds like she got laid," Margie guffawed when Hunter got back to Atlanta later that night.

"That occurred to me on the ride back. I guess I just didn't want to realize it while I was there," Hunter replied, the phone trapped in the crook of his neck as he peeled off his socks.

"I think it's hysterical," Margie said and started laughing again.

"Oh, laugh a minute. Now I have to worry about who's porking my mom."

"Give me a break, Hunter. If I hadn't gotten any dick since the Stone Age, I'd be cranky too," she said and laughed.

"Your compassion just thrills me, Margie, but she can't just up and change on me like this."

"Poor wittle Hunter," she cooed across the phone. "He sounds jealous."

"I'm not jealous. I'm...annoyed. She never even told me."

"Jealous," Margie countered immediately. "And what if it's a woman?"

It was Hunter's turn to laugh. "Shit. No way. You forget this is the same woman who brought a hooker home for me the day after I told her I was gay. She thought she could change me back or some shit."

"Hey, I never said your mom wasn't a little tapped. And what are you bitching about?" Margie questioned him. "You said you wanted total freedom, now you got it. Stop your whining."

He chewed his lip. "Do you think she's finally gotten over

the idea that she caused my sexuality?"

Margie clucked her tongue on the other end of the phone. They'd had many a discussion about his domineering mother and no father in the house causing Hunter to be gay. But he thought it all a bunch of homophobic bullshit made up by straight people who couldn't even figure out how to stay married in the first place. Nobody had caused the little woody he'd gotten when he was eleven and smelled the sweet sweat of one of his closest friends.

"Hell, you would know better than I would," Margie answered. "I think she just doesn't want to be alone anymore. The frigid bitch thing wasn't working. She doesn't have you hanging around anymore. So, why not try something different? You know, live a little."

"How many years of therapy did that response take to develop?"

"About twenty, smartass, but you're getting it for free. Christ, you're such a whiner. You've finally got your freedom, now do something with it."

She hung up and Hunter put the phone down, his fingers strumming on the arm of the couch.

Chapter 5

One week later, the downstairs buzzer sounded and startled Hunter while he was on the phone with Margie. They were discussing some of the wording on one of the manuscripts and the characteristics the voice needed to sound authentic. Hunter hadn't ordered takeout, so the buzzer could only mean one of his neighbors had locked themselves out again.

"How is it that my blind ass can find my key every time, but the sightlings in this apartment building can't find their own frigging house key?" he growled, speaking more to himself than Margie.

"That was your door?" she asked.

"The downstairs buzzer," he corrected. "It's probably one of the neighbors again. I don't know how the hell I became the official door opener in this dump. Hang on." He went to the panel and keyed the mic. He knew the reason behind his neighbors' laziness. Hunter could recognize all their voices and wouldn't open the door to anyone he didn't know. Through his own fault, he'd somehow become the vetter of lost key vocalists.

Press the button and see if the blind man lets you in. What the fuck was that? Or is that just me being sensitive? he asked himself.

"Yes?" he demanded, letting his annoyance be known.

"Hunter?"

The voice fell over him like a spell, like a sachet of rosemary, citrus, and the tangy foreign texture of myrrh. He instantly remembered smelling a fragrance which Napoléon supposedly wore that was on a scratch and sniff in an old National Geographic when he was a kid. Frank's voice brought that memory, and the longing he'd had for him since their first tryst together.

"It's Frank, I'm sorry. I don't mean to barge in on you. I...uh, can I come up?"

"Yeah, sure," Hunter answered immediately. "Hang on. I'll buzz you up." He hit the buzzer and raced back to the phone as fast as he could.

"It's Frank, I've got to go. He's coming up," he told Margie quickly.

When he and Lydia originally checked out this apartment, Lydia had insisted on the first floor. This, of course, made him demand anything but. But after taking the second-floor apartment and trudging groceries up and down the stairs a few times, he realized how his own obstinacy had thwarted convenience. He'd been more than a little pissed at himself. But this time those stairs were working in his favor.

"Who's Frank?" Margie asked.

"From last week."

"The prostitute? Hunter, don't you dare..."

He cut her off and put the phone down when the knock came. Taking a deep breath to calm his sudden nervousness, he went to the door. As he grabbed the knob, he licked his lips, wondering why he was more anxious now than when he'd brought Frank home the first time. At least he knew the apartment was clean. The woman his mother hired to come once a week kept the place spotless, even though she was a spy.

"Hi," Hunter said as he opened the door. He could smell Frank immediately in the waft of air that came in. He smelled manly, muscular, and fucking hot. Hunter wanted him right in the doorway.

"I'm sorry to pop up like this," Frank apologized again. "I...here." He gently took Hunter's wrist, brought his hand up, and filled it with an open envelope.

Hunter was pretty sure it wasn't coupons or a bunch of love letters, so that meant it could only be one thing, his money. "What's this?"

"Call it a refund. I...let's just call it a refund," Frank replied.

Hunter's emotions went into instant turmoil. Did Frank consider last week a mercy fuck? But that's not what his articulation said. There seemed to be more in Frank's tone than pity and he wanted to know what it was. "Why don't you come in?" Hunter stepped back and opened the door further, trying to keep the curious agitation from his voice.

"I probably shouldn't."

Shouldn't wasn't no. It was, I really want to, but don't want to ask.

"Please, come in," Hunter insisted. "We can have a drink and you can explain this. Besides, you have to tell me what the denominations are so I don't get screwed when I use them." He held out the envelope and shook it at Frank for emphasis.

"I've already folded the bills in the right denominations for you. But there's nothing to explain, I just..." Frank trailed off, an odd texture in his voice. It was as if it was a foreign emotion pushing his words out; something foreign enough to him that he wasn't comfortable with it himself.

"Come in anyway," Hunter pressed him, curious about his reason for returning the money and even more curious about how Frank knew how to fold the money correctly.

"By the way, my name's not Frank, it's Dillon," he said as he came in. "My real name is Dillon."

"Dillon," Hunter repeated, after a stunned pause. He liked it much better than Frank, but he'd assumed Dillon had given him a false name anyway. What sensible prostitute wouldn't? "Hmm, truth and money," Hunter said as he closed and locked the door. "Did you have a rough week?"

"Something like that."

Hunter cocked his head to the side, hoping Dillon would sit down and explain himself. But he didn't. He stood in the middle of the living room fidgeting with his hands. Hunter could hear the nervous rasp of his fingers as they clenched and unclenched. "Please sit. Can I get you a drink?"

"No, I only drink when I'm working. This was personal. I mean...I hadn't planned on coming up. I was just...well." He blew out a breath, frustrated with his apparent lack of finesse. "I was just going to put the money in your mailbox, but they're inside and locked."

Hunter ran a hand through his hair. Dillon sounded like he was ready to sprint for the door, and not at all like the confident man he'd been last week. "How about a Coke instead?" Hunter asked.

"No, but thanks anyway."

Hunter sat on the couch and patted it. A moment later, he felt Dillon's weight drop down like a child ordered to behave himself at a family gathering.

"So, what's up?" Hunter asked as the phone rang. "Hang on a sec."

"Hello, Margie," he said as he picked up the phone. He knew she'd call back.

"Goddamn it, Hunter! If that guy's not out of there in two minutes I'm calling the cops," Margie squawked.

"Margie, shut up. All right? I'm fine. I'll call you tomorrow." Hunter hung up and put the phone down.

"That's not the same friend from last week, is it?" Dillon asked.

"Yes, she worries. Hot stranger, blind man…you know." He shrugged. "Now, again. What's up with this?" he asked, tapping the envelope against his leg.

"Well, to be honest, I don't trick. I mean I do, but not like... I'm trying to say I don't hustle strangers on the street. I work for an agency. Last week was a throwback to a history I abandoned a long time ago," Dillon said entirely too fast.

"So why not just keep the money?" Hunter asked, perplexed.

He heard Dillon's coat rustle as if he'd shuffled in distinct discomfort at the question.

"I don't know. It just seemed…right. I guess I felt guilty."

This wasn't true. Hunter could hear it in his voice immediately. What he heard was tinged with regret, not guilt; and though some might dispute the hair of difference between them, Hunter found them to be entirely separate mindsets.

He reached up slowly and sought out and caressed Dillon's face, feeling his tense frown as he swiped his thumb across Dillon's cheek. He also heard a small intake of breath, the stubble on Dillon's chin betraying the slight shiver his touch caused. "What's this really about?" he asked as he moved his hand around and cupped the side of Dillon's neck. "We don't know each other well enough that you have to lie. Just spit it out. I'd rather you be honest than feed me bullshit."

Dillon was quiet for a moment. Hunter took his hand back, noting how Dillon's breath became more measured before he spoke.

"I…sometimes I just need a human body next to me. You know? Someone who wants me for me, not just because he's paying the agency. When I work there's no affection, there's just the trick."

"Just skin," Hunter interjected.

"Yeah. Anyway, that's why I brought the money back. Last week was…it was nice."

The couch shifted as Dillon shrugged or moved his hands about, Hunter couldn't tell which it was. But nice wasn't the word he would've used. Nice was missionary sex; nice was a nun going frolicking where she shouldn't; nice was a twenty-year married couple.

What they'd experienced wasn't nice. It was intensely erotic and a great fuck, but he could hear Dillon desperately trying to deny it for some reason.

"Well, maybe you should be paying me then," Hunter quipped.

Dillon laughed and Hunter heard his anxiety deflate somewhat. "Loneliness isn't a crime," Hunter said. "You of all people should understand that."

"Yeah, well... I've got to go," Dillon said as he stood up quickly, obviously embarrassed that his profession was central to Hunter's perceptions.

"You could stay," Hunter blurted. It wasn't just the idea of more great sex, though that was definitely a part of it. Hunter wanted Dillon's company. The courage and honesty he'd shown in coming back made Hunter want him that much more. Dillon hadn't owed him an explanation. Yet, he seemed... genuine and honestly lonely – maybe even as lonely as Hunter was.

"That's probably not a good idea," Dillon said slowly.

Hunter tilted his head and smirked. He had to lighten this up. "I'll give you a freebie." Christ, now I sound desperate, Hunter thought. But when Dillon chuckled, he realized Dillon wanted to stay as much as he needed him to.

Then why does this feel like that awkward moment before sex with a high school prom date? Hunter asked himself. "Have you eaten yet? I'm starving. You like Chinese?" Hunter asked quickly, thinking maybe another tactic would work better. Food was always a neutral subject. It was why most relationships started and ended in restaurants.

"Love it," Dillon answered.

"Good. Tell you what. I'll set the table. You call and surprise me. It's the third button down on the speed dialer," Hunter told him, indicating the phone on the end table. "They're just around the corner and I eat pretty much anything."

Dillon seemed to think about it for a minute before he answered. "Okay, but I'll buy."

"Fair enough." Hunter went to the kitchen and heard Dillon phone the restaurant while he was taking down the plates. He didn't pay attention because he was too busy marveling at the fact that it was the first time in months that a second plate had left the shelf. *Is my life really that pathetic?*

The last time he'd reached for a second plate had been for his mother's quarterly visit. It struck him as ironic that he was pulling down a plate for a prostitute. He shook his head at himself, but stopped and tuned in when he realized Dillon was speaking Chinese.

And the more Hunter listened and thought about that oddity, the more he realized another peculiarity. Dillon had been immediately comfortable with his blindness, which Hunter may have taken more notice of had he been a little less horny when they'd first met. But the simple fact was that last week had just been good, hot sex which he'd desperately needed. He hadn't been paying attention to anything except getting their clothes off. But now that he thought about it…

"In the kitchen," Dillon announced as he came in. "Is there anything I can do to help?"

Typically, a seeing person not used to moving around a blind man while within the house wouldn't know to broadcast his to and fro activities. It was done for safety as well as common courtesy. But sightlings sometimes had an odd reaction to the simple courtesy because they weren't used to publicizing their movements, if they were even aware of such a courtesy at all.

Hmm, Hunter thought. Dillon just kept getting more and more mysterious. "I've got it," he answered, "but thanks. Were you speaking Chinese?" he asked as he reached into the drawer for a couple of forks.

Dillon's response seemed shy and a little self-conscious. "I learned it as a teenager. It's a bit rough, but I can communicate."

"Impressive." Hunter heard the movement of cloth and thought Dillon might have shrugged again. He was definitely uncomfortable with the topic and it made Hunter wonder why. Knowledge was nothing to be ashamed of.

"Not really," Dillon answered. "Survival prompted it."

Again, Dillon's reluctance to add anything more to the conversation seemed obvious, so Hunter didn't press, but now he really had Hunter's curiosity. How many Chinese speaking escorts could there be in Atlanta?

"Sounds like an interesting story, maybe you could tell me

some time," he said as he made his way to the table and put the settings down. He paused at one of the chairs and rested his hands on the back of it. He heard Dillon follow him to the table and spoke to the light whisper of Dillon's breath a few feet away. "Can I ask you a question?"

"Um, sure. Go ahead," Dillon answered with a small smile in his voice.

"Why is that funny?" Hunter asked, his tone brusque.

"Because it sounds defensive already," Dillon replied.

"Yeah, I guess it did come out like that. Sorry. But, I do have to be a little careful."

"I understand. What's your question?" Dillon asked.

"The money…" Hunter frowned and took a breath, not sure if he wanted an honest answer to his next question. "It's not like last week was a mercy fuck or something, was it?"

"Would that bother you?"

"Honestly, yes. The sex was great so I might get over it pretty quick." He laughed. "But even so, if you haven't guessed already, I'm not into the poor, blind guy shit. All that does is piss me off."

Dillon chuckled as he moved closer. A wave of his peculiar fragrance fell over Hunter and he felt a gentle and tentative touch as Dillon cupped his jaw in the palm of his hand.

"The sex was pretty great," Dillon said. "But no, it wasn't a mercy fuck. And no, I don't feel sorry for the little blind boy, not at all. And so you understand, I've never come back to a client's house uninvited. And I've never returned cash before either. Never."

Hunter rolled his face into Dillon's palm, soaking in the strong, masculine scent of his body. He was like an aphrodisiac and Hunter only caught half of his words. "Is someone in your family blind?" he asked, enjoying the intimate familiarity Dillon had with his blindness minus all the hang-ups and curiosities.

Dillon quickly pulled his hand away. "My cousin was blind."

Was. Hunter stored his response and the preceding reaction away for another time, perhaps when they were more comfortable with each other.

At the moment, Dillon's voice was like honey and sex and chocolate all rolled into one. But his inflection suggested that this particular subject was laced with a touch of the taboo. Hunter's curiosity was definitely aroused, but the thought of a repeat performance of last week's sex seemed much more alluring than chit-chatting about some unspoken but obvious wounds.

"So if I offered you a beer, would that turn this into a professional visit?" Hunter asked.

Dillon sniggered and it made Hunter realize that laughter, genuine laughter, and not just snark, didn't seem to be a big part of his life. He wondered why that was.

"No, I could go for a beer," Dillon answered. "You want me to grab them?"

"Sure," Hunter said as he made his way back to the couch and sat down. He listened as Dillon popped two beers and brought them out to the living room.

"I like your apartment," Dillon told him as he came to the couch.

"Thanks. After my mother got over the idea that it was too dangerous for me to be living in the big city all by my lonesome, she wanted it to look nice 'for my trysts'."

"So she knows you're gay?" Dillon asked, sipping on his beer as he sat.

"Yeah, there wasn't too much she could do about it. Once this little bird was out of the nest, she lost."

There was an awkward silence between them as they sipped their beers. For some reason, an old self-conscious memory of Lydia admonishing him about rocking while he sat popped into Hunter's head. He pushed himself back into the couch as the silence stretched and took another sip of the beer, hoping the food would arrive quickly.

"Can I be extraordinarily honest?" Dillon asked suddenly.

"Sure."

"You're hot as fuck and I'm dying to get you into bed again."

The beer halted halfway to Hunter's mouth as his head snapped to the sound of Dillon's voice.

"I don't know what it is, but I've been rock hard since I got here and I don't think I can wait through all this oral foreplay," Dillon told him.

For a very brief second, Hunter wondered if that was the hustler talking or the man. Then he realized that he really didn't give a shit either way, he just wanted Dillon naked again. He felt along the couch until his hand bumped up against Dillon's leg. When he slid it up Dillon's thigh and grasped the hard flesh between his legs, Dillon instantly groaned with a cinnamon lust that drove Hunter wild.

"I wasn't lying," Dillon panted as Hunter started kneading and stroking him through the fabric of his jeans.

"I see that, but the food…" Hunter said, hearing his own voice growing thick with need.

Dillon gasped as Hunter gripped him more forcefully. "I ordered it for a 7:30 delivery," he confessed.

"What time is it?" Hunter asked, unwilling to pull his hands away and check his watch. He knew it wasn't that late. He'd only been talking with Margie for about forty minutes before the downstairs buzzer had sounded.

"5:14," Dillon answered.

Sly as hell, something I'll have to watch for in the future, Hunter thought. "Let's go in the bedroom," he said immediately after.

Dillon grabbed Hunter's hand from his groin, put their beers on the table, and led him into the bedroom. Turning Hunter in his arms, he gently pressed the back of Hunter's legs against the side of the bed and folded him down across it, following closely as Hunter lay down.

"I want to kiss you," Dillon rasped, his hot breath only centimeters from Hunter's face.

"I want you raw this time, no shower," Hunter panted back.

He could feel himself turning into Dillon's kiss without any worry that he was about to kiss his nose. Dillon seemed so natural to him, so…in tune.

Dillon dove into him and pressed his lips against Hunter as if he were trying to push him through the bed. His tongue was a hot dagger in Hunter's mouth, his hands ran over Hunter's ribs and shoulders like he was massaging Hunter's skin through his t-shirt.

Goddamn, he tastes good, Hunter thought.

He put his hands on either side of Dillon's head and pulled him closer, harder. He would've gladly crawled right into Dillon's mouth if he could've. He could feel the heat of Dillon's body and the light perspiration on his temples already. His cock was a thrusting bulge of jean-covered flesh between them and Hunter wanted it unleashed.

When Dillon reached down and started to slide Hunter's t-shirt up, Hunter reached out and ripped Dillon's buttoned shirt open so that he clearly understood his deepest instant desire. This was to be man sex. "Take me," Hunter demanded after pushing Dillon's lips back an inch.

Everyone had treated him gently his entire life, like he was a fragile little butterfly who would break if handled too rough. That attitude enraged him. It was even worse when it happened with the few lovers he'd brought home, as if he was too delicate to fuck.

Hunter wanted Dillon to fuck him like a man. He wanted Dillon hard and thrusting and he wanted to be taken. He wanted to feel Dillon explode inside of him; wanted to smell Dillon's balls as he gnawed on them; wanted to wince as Dillon chewed on his nipples. He wanted to taste the sweat at Dillon's temples while he fucked him like a whore.

And Dillon immediately understood. He pushed Hunter's t-shirt up, slipped his hands around Hunter's waist, and fell upon his chest, chewing on Hunter's tender nipples the moment they were in his mouth.

Hunter could only groan and arch up to Dillon's hot mouth as he slammed his hands back to the bed and gripped the sheets on either side of him. He could smell the cigarettes in Dillon's hair and suddenly he wanted to ride Dillon's cock while he smoked one. He wanted to drag Dillon back to the couch naked as hell, straddle him, and lick Dillon's chest while Dillon smoked one of those filthy cigarettes in his house and rammed that big circumcised cock up his ass.

Dillon pulled off of Hunter's chest in a slow, succulent suck that puckered out the nipple he had in his mouth. He dropped his hands to Hunter's jeans and began tugging at the buttons like a cat pawing at a birdcage. Neither of them could get their clothing off fast enough, no matter how hard they tried.

"Want you," Dillon panted as he reached down and stripped Hunter's pants and jockeys off.

Hunter pulled his t-shirt over his head and heard the buttons on Dillon's shirt pop off into the room as he reached forward and ripped the remainder of Dillon's shirt from his chest. He heard Dillon's shoes thud and then Dillon's belt jingle before his pants dropped to join everything else. Dillon was crawling over him a quick moment later. The tip of his cock leaving a trail as Dillon crawled back up to meet Hunter's mouth.

"How the fuck are you doing this to me?" Dillon demanded; the husky ache of his voice making Hunter wet with the strength of his need.

"You smell like prison," Hunter whispered as he slipped his arms around Dillon's waist and pulled his firm, round ass to him.

And he did, Dillon smelled masculine and hot and scary and scarred. It was all rolled into one. He smelled of feet and armpits and ball sweat and Hunter wanted to taste every single one of those flavors. He wanted to mingle with them and fuck in a sweaty, senseless lust.

Dillon drew back. He paused for a moment at Hunter's choice of words but then dove at his mouth again. His tongue went deep in Hunter's throat, his lips mashed hard and unforgiving against his Hunter's lips like he wanted to taste those words over and over. You smell like prison.

Hunter pushed him back just enough so he could speak. "Fuck me," he commanded again.

"Ugggnnn." It was all he could utter when Dillon lifted his legs, lubed him, and speared him. He thrust his cock deep into Hunter's ass until Hunter felt the full weight of his shaft buried within him.

The seconds Dillon had spent applying lube had been too long, but this…this wiped those seconds away in an instant. He could feel the mushroomed head, the thick veins, the length and breadth of Dillon's cock. He'd wanted it so bad that it pushed him right to the brink of an orgasm before they even started.

***

Dillon paused, allowing Hunter to feel his fullness before he began moving with small thrusts. He could tell he already had Hunter on the cusp of orgasm, but his own lust wouldn't allow that yet. He craved Hunter like he had no another man. He yearned to be inside him; ached to taste his lips; hungered to hear him howl for more. But he wanted Hunter to desire more than that. He longed for intimacy and coveted Hunter's fluttering pulse. Secretly, he hoped Hunter would gasp with words that were more than sex.

***

"Give it to me," Hunter whimpered. He'd sought to be forceful and manly with those words, but they came out like a plea.

He wanted Dillon deep inside him. His ass tingled and his cock throbbed with his urgent desire. He needed it like he needed air. He wanted to be bred and used and fucked. Not fucked like he was fragile, but fucked like he meant something – fucked like his blindness wasn't a thing that stood between them, even if it was only for this one night.

A howl escaped his lips as Dillon pulled back and began hammering into him. He could feel drops of Dillon's lust-filled sweat scorching his skin and leaned forward to lick it from Dillon's chest. He still needed more. He thrust himself against Dillon, lifting his legs higher into the air as he forced his hole down Dillon's shaft.

The sound of their sex was a hard knocking of wet flesh as they slammed against each other with complete abandon.

Not one of Hunter's few lovers had ever brought him to orgasm just by fucking him. But as Dillon's cock started to swell, and as his thrusts got shorter and deeper, Hunter felt it rise up within him. He felt it grow inside like the swell of an immutable current in the ocean. He grabbed Dillon and dug his nails into his back, his claws coming out like a cat's as he rose into the heat of Dillon's lust.

He pulled himself from the mattress, the full weight of his body sliding down Dillon's length. One bite on his neck and Dillon's body went rigid, his first spurt so hot inside Hunter it felt like fire – a liquid smattering of lust against the walls of his ass. He came instantly; a thick, ropy stream bursting between them as Dillon finished and filled him with his seed. They both cried out as they fell back to the bed.

"That was incredible," Dillon gasped, turning into Hunter's ear as he lay on top of him.

Hunter nodded. He couldn't speak. That, he thought, was what sex was supposed to be like.

Dillon's cock was still hard and buried deep. "Okay?" he asked as gently he stroked Hunter's hair.

"Yes," Hunter answered, his breath still short. He locked his legs around Dillon's calves, not quite ready to let him go. "Yes," he whispered a second time.

Dillon kissed him, exploring Hunter's mouth and cupping the sides of his head so that he couldn't escape. "Did we really just fuck and cum within five minutes like two teenagers?" he asked when he pulled back, the amusement in his voice contagious.

Hunter nodded with a grin. "I don't ever remember anything like that as a teenager. Is that normal?" he rasped. "That wasn't like last week at all, not even close. It was damn near angelic."

Dillon chuckled. "Angelic sex, I thought it was more the demonic version." He let out a long breath. "And no, it's never been like that before. Not for me."

Dillon rolled and laid down by Hunter's side as Hunter curled into him. Dillon's arm came around him like they were old lovers. "You know, this is the first time I can honestly say I need a cigarette," Dillon said.

"Are we done already?" Hunter asked, a small moue of disappointment not entirely hidden from his voice. His hand reached down to find the plumpness of Dillon's cock once more.

Dillon laughed and kissed his nose. "No. This is just a pause. We've got at least another hour to go before the food gets here. And I want some of that first," Dillon growled as he grabbed Hunter's cock. He rolled Hunter on top of him and sought Hunter's mouth as his legs opened and wrapped around Hunter's waist.

Hunter had no objections.

Chapter 6

The next morning, Dillon stood in his condo watching the skyline brighten. He'd done it. He'd broken the cardinal rule of prostitution. He'd fallen for a trick, returned to the trick's house unbidden, and, worst of all, he'd returned the money. For that alone he could be castrated upon the kur-garru altar of Ishtar and exiled into normality, or worse, forced into hetero sex.

He blew out a breath, irritated. He tried to tell himself it was just mild infatuation. But, that wasn't true. He'd been with Hunter twice. But, inexplicably, he couldn't get the guy out of his head. No matter what he did, where he went, or who he talked to, Hunter was in his thoughts – from the scent of his body to the curve of his ass, Hunter was with him. It was driving him fucking crazy.

He didn't believe in love at first sight or any of the other crap romance movies liked to crow about. How could you meet a complete stranger and just know they were the one? Ridiculous.

How many times had one of his tricks fallen over themselves gawking at him? How many times had they professed faith and love and money and anything else they thought he might need to make the attraction mutual?

And then, on his side of the game, there was the hustler makes it big myth. It was a common delusion for call boys about how you met the rich trick of your dreams, fell in love and made it out of the business. That shit never happened either. All the male escorts he knew had turned into graying old wannabes, drugged out meth heads or were dead. None had made a clean break from the business. Not one.

But it was supposed to be different for him? Don't buy it, he told himself. Hope was a fool's game. He'd learn that lesson early and well.

He pushed his brooding away as he turned from the window and found himself reminiscing about Shawn Langford. Shawn had brought him to this point in his life, to this train of thought. Shawn had been an elderly client who had watched the entire cadre of his closest friends die in the AIDS epidemic. It was something he'd never gotten over.

One day, on a whim he attributed to the winning of a pair of theater tickets, Shawn had called Roland, the owner of the escort agency Dillon worked for. He asked about a possible dinner companion. No sex was involved. It was just dinner and the theater. He claimed he couldn't go alone and protocol dictated that he couldn't blow off the event without a tangible excuse. Dillon happened to get the hookup, one of his first at Roland's secretive escort agency, and that night at dinner they'd hit it off immediately.

Six years and many Saturday dinner and theater dates later, Shawn sat him down and told him he was dying of pancreatic cancer. In six weeks, he was dead and Dillon was opening an envelope from a big Atlanta law firm that said he was the sole beneficiary of everything Shawn owned. He got the condo he stood in, a car and enough money to live on for the next ten years. If he invested wisely and lived carefully, he had enough to live on for the rest of his life.

The day he received that letter was only the third time since he'd left home that he sat down and had a serious cry. Shawn had become a friend over the years, but he'd forbidden Dillon to be with him at the end. He went to the hospital alone and died alone.

In the letter that accompanied the will, he made the written point that he didn't want the same to happen to Dillon, hence the exclusion from his final moments. He urged Dillon to get out of the escort business and make a life of his own with someone he cared about, not just with geriatric clients like himself. It was the most unselfish thing anyone had ever done for him.

Dillon had never discussed his past with Shawn. He didn't discuss it with any customer. But he and Shawn had talked at length about Shawn's past, and it wasn't too far from his own. If you didn't count the fact that Dillon had spent his early years on the street eating out of garbage cans until a Chinese immigrant named Shu-shu had taken pity on him.

Shawn had never spent time on the streets. He'd come from a wealthy and devoutly Catholic family up north who disowned after he'd come out in college. But Shawn had expected their reaction and had already built a safety net for himself. He was no fool. He had a full scholarship and plenty of employment offers. So when he walked out of college with a degree in chemical engineering, he had multiple spots waiting for him. He took the one that moved him farthest from his family, knowing the money would come his way once he had more work experience. He never saw or spoke to his family again and that had seemed to suit him fine. Then he was dead, and Dillon was getting a certified letter. Dillon still felt the weight of that day on him.

He'd tried quitting the biz and had talked to a shrink about it at some length after Shawn's death. But the doctor wanted to get into all that Freudian hate-your-mommy shit and he'd never gone back. But he'd never actually left either. He was always on the doctor's couch now – always self-evaluating his motives, constantly looking back, and continuously worrying forward.

He didn't have to hustle anymore, but he kept at it anyway. He didn't know anything else and had no other skills. He was great at reading people and excellent with languages. Hell, he had been an honors student before his parents chucked him out. But none of that equaled a job, skills, or a history of a job. Quietly, he was afraid that he'd never be anything more than a high-priced whore. And in the end, his decision to continue had come down to the realization that he couldn't imagine trying to run off to start a new life.

A new life would begin with a lie about where he came from and what he'd done to get there. After the first lie, he'd be stuck fabricating more lies. His life would fill with a constant worry about who might find out about his past. He could see the complexity of the lies getting deeper and deeper. And after living a new lie every single night since he was sixteen, he recognized that a beginning based on such a lie was doomed to failure before it even began.

In the end, he didn't leave the sex trade. Instead, he told himself that his financial security gave him the ability to select his clients more carefully. But he'd always been able to do that. And yet…he didn't, and he still wasn't happy. Not even close.

And now?

Now, there was a blind man he'd stumbled across who wouldn't leave his head – a man who exuded confidence and lust and genuine affability. And Dillon didn't know why he couldn't stop thinking about him. He didn't understand it. He didn't want it. And he damned sure didn't like it. But he was unable to stop it.

"What am I going to do with you, Hunter?" he asked his empty condo. He looked down and realized that he'd gone to the fridge and grabbed a beer. He glanced at the clock, shook his head, and emptied the beer in the sink. Hunter had his head so screwed up he couldn't even pick an appropriate morning beverage.

He filled the kettle, turned it on, and was lost in thought until he heard it whistling. "What am I going to do with me?" he asked out loud.

A thought came to him as he poured the water into his cup and watched it flow over the tea bag. The steam rose with a light, fresh fragrance and gave him an idea. It didn't answer his question. But he thought that maybe he should just go with the flow and let the questions answer themselves. Eventually, these issues would work themselves out, or they wouldn't.

He nodded and went in search of his phone.

Chapter 7

"Dillon?" Hunter called out. He reached over and felt the empty bed. It was cool. He sat up and listened for movement, but there was no noise in the apartment at all. "Fuck," he groaned and flopped back to the pillow.

Had he done something wrong? Was Dillon upset or was he just playing him for a fool?

Last night, he'd been thinking they had potential. Dillon had returned with what seemed like heartfelt warmth and refunded his money. If that wasn't some kind of indication of genuine interest, then what was it? And then there was the sex… Jesus, the sex.

He frowned. He hated head games. "I'll just wait and see what happens," he told himself, as if it would make him more confident about the situation. But that wasn't going to work. He wasn't the type of guy who hung around hoping the phone would ring. "Fuck it," he barked as he rolled out of bed. "I've got too much to do to worry about this shit."

Today, he had a meeting with the attorney of a previous client who wanted to get an old contract changed. (That wasn't happening.) He also had a four-hour studio session with Margie and three new cast members. There were a bunch of potential new voices to listen to. And he wanted to put in a few extra hours at the dojo. The day was full and he had little time for antics of the heart.

***

Six hours later, Hunter was sitting in his rented studio space listening to some southern belle wannabe crone on like she was casting for the audio version of Gone with the Wind. "Next!" he bellowed.

"Hunter, chill out. You're scaring off our potential help," Margie complained. She was sitting beside him in the control room.

"She sucks," Hunter griped.

"Yeah, she does, but it's a casting call for a low-paying, shit job. We're not booking backups for Pavarotti. Chill."

She paused for a moment and Hunter could sense her eyes prying at him. Even blind, he could feel the weight of her stare.

"What the hell's wrong with you?" she finally asked. "It wasn't just that meeting with the lawyers."

"Can you believe the balls?" Hunter demanded, off on the tangent conversation they'd had earlier. "He wanted me to just tear up the contract and hand them over all the rights so Donnie wouldn't be forking out cash to so many different people. Like that's my fucking problem. I never told him to hire two separate agents after he started making a little money."

"Our contracts are rock solid," Margie reiterated her earlier words.

"I know it. And they know it too," Hunter fumed. "I'm just trying to figure out what the meeting was even for. Waste of my freaking time."

"They're just feeling you out." Margie tried to console him

as the next person came up to the microphone and started reading the script they'd prepared. She saw Hunter's interest peak at the man's voice and got quiet.

"Him, yes," Hunter said after listening for a few minutes. "Not for this project, though. Give him a retainer contract. I think he'd be good for that new one Sax brought us. I'm not sure which character yet, but I like the stones in his voice." He listened closely for a few more seconds. "Give him one of those inflection tapes too. Have him do a demo and see if he can alter his vocalizations enough to round out his tonation. If he can, he'd be good for more than one or two characters."

"Okay," she answered, her pen jittering across her notepad.

There was a tap at the control room door followed by the thump of heavy boots as Margie waved their new voice talent off to the side. Hunter turned to meet the sound.

"Got a package for Hunter, no last name," the man with the boots said. His voice was crisp, efficient, and entirely business. Likely an excellent employee, Hunter thought. Smells squeaky clean too. Masculine, he added with a wry smile showing his internal assessment. He pointed at Margie without saying a word.

Margie signed for it and waited for the man leave before she spoke. "Why do you always do that?" she demanded. "You bitch about independence and then pawn people off to me when you're right here."

"Plausible deniability," Hunter answered. "'I never got any letter, your honor.' Besides, if it's a bomb from a disgruntled writer, why would I want it?"

"Gee, thanks."

"What is it?" Hunter asked when she opened the box. An aroma suddenly filled the control room. It was a beautiful bouquet, like a mixture of milk and honey or some kind of spun candy. He inhaled again as it swirled around him. Wow, if I could capture that in sound, he thought.

"It's a plant," Margie answered skeptically. "It looks like a bunch of sticks with a flower on top. Oh, wait. Let me read the description..."

"Oh," she said after a moment.

"What?" Hunter demanded, intrigue coloring his voice.

"It's called, get this now, Queen of the Night," Margie told him. "It only blooms once a year, if that, and it uses its fragrance to attract pollinators rather than attracting them by sight. The card says it was shipped when it started blooming so you could appreciate the fragrance."

She laughed and looked at Hunter. "This guy is slick. I'll give him that."

"Is there another card?" Hunter asked.

"No," she said, dragging out her reply. "I assume you know who it's from. It's not like either of us has a stable of boyfriends."

Hunter sneered at her. Obviously, only one person could have sent it. But how did Dillon know where he was going to be? Had he mentioned the studio as they wound down the night and fell into a blissful sleep? He didn't think so...

"Tell me it wasn't the prostitute." Margie prodded.

"He's an escort, not a prostitute, and his name is Dillon."

"Oh, excuse me. Nice to see you're on a first-name basis, though," Margie needled him further. "Wait, I thought you said his name was Frank."

Hunter made a grunting noise that didn't quite dismiss his refusal to acknowledge her taunt. "He left early this morning without saying goodbye," he admitted. "I thought…" He trailed off into silence, the words having slipped out due more to his own frustration at the meeting with Donnie's attorney than with Dillon. At least that's what he told himself. "This must be his way of apologizing."

She believed that about as much as he did. "You thought he duped you into sex," Margie announced, disputing his claim. She shook her head. "It's a part of the routine, Hunter. It keeps you coming back for more. Like a crackhead, or in your case, just the crack." She laughed at her own joke. "He gets all up inside your head and all of a sudden you're buying him cars and thinking its romance while he's screwing someone else on your off nights."

"He gave my money back," Hunter told her without the least bit of humor in his voice.

She went silent. "Really?"

"Yes, really. We fucked, had dinner at my place, and then fucked for a few more hours."

"So, let me take a wild guess here. Now you're under the impression that you're building a relationship that's not based on money. Is that the delusion you have?"

"I don't know. It's complicated," Hunter answered, a vague wish resonating somewhere in his words.

"Complicated? Pfft. You're already hooked. Who are you trying to BS?" Margie asked. "So, am I going to get to meet this guy or what?" she added as an afterthought. "Assuming of course, you do have something more than just sex."

Hunter paused for a moment and scratched at his chin. "No, I don't think so. Not yet."

"Why the hell not?"

"Because you're right, it hasn't progressed anywhere. I don't even know him myself yet," Hunter replied.

"But you'd like to know him more, even though you've never been on an actual date or anything," Margie said.

He shrugged one shoulder, not willing to admit it out loud.

"Good lord, you are such a drama queen," Margie replied.

"Bitter fag hag."

"Drama queen," Margie retorted before she got quiet.

"Don't do this to yourself, Hunter. Okay? I'm saying this as a friend," Margie offered, her tone softer.

"Do what?"

"Fall for this guy."

"Come on, Margie..."

"Hunter, this guy's a hustler, that's what he does. He fucks people for money. Don't do that to yourself."

"You're putting way too much into this, Margie. It was fun, but you know, I've got a life."

"I'm just telling you, as a friend," Margie said.

"Okay, Lydia, no more pricey cock for me."

"That's not what I meant and you know it," Margie snapped back at him. She was as defensive about being compared to Lydia as Hunter was about living a lifestyle unfettered by other people's opinions.

Hunter knew she meant well, but he was a grown man who happened to be blind. He wasn't an imbecile unable to take care of himself and he detested being treated as if he couldn't run his own goddamned life. Not that Margie was trying to run anything. But her persistent cautions seemed to emphasize his blindness more than show how much she valued their friendship. And that irked him no matter how she tried to rationalize it.

"Okay, so you didn't mean it that way. Can we get off my non-existent love life and focus on business here?" Hunter snarled.

"I just don't want to have to chase this guy down with a butcher knife," Margie told him.

"Fair enough," Hunter answered with a small smile, but the smile was only an external thing. Inside, all he could think about was the sound and the smell and the blood of Dillon. The feel of his arms, the breadth of his chest, how he nibbled as he wrapped himself around Hunter was like a soft vice of hard passion. He was a mallet banging on things well beyond, and deep inside, that place where the darkness of Hunter's missing vision could not go.

He was hooked already. He knew it and he knew Margie knew it, and that's what made it so damned exasperating.

And then there was something like this, a well thought out gift; something which spoke volumes without stating anything obvious. But Margie was right; Dillon was a prostitute and could be out fucking another client right now for all he knew. And shit, if he ever told Margie that their sex was unsafe last night... The thought of even attempting that conversation made him cringe. She'd go ballistic on him.

He felt the numb burn of melancholy run through him and couldn't explain it. He and Dillon weren't a couple and had no potential to be. What would a hot stud like Dillon see in someone like him anyway? The most he could hope for was that he'd be Dillon's little side project – something he could claim as his own while tossing Hunter a mercy fuck now and again. Hunter wouldn't be a part of Dillon's daily life, just a fringe benefit – the lonely blind freak who liked manly smells and kinky sex.

He knew a relationship would never work. The mere thought of Dillon sleeping with someone else already felt like hot pepper on his tongue. How much worse it'd be if he let his heart get involved and then woke up to a cold space like he had this morning?

"Thinking you should just keep it about sex?" Margie asked quietly.

"Something like that," he answered in a long exhale of frustration, irked that Margie knew him so well that she could plug right into his private thoughts.

"Big risk opening yourself up, feeling vulnerable."

"What the fuck would you know about vulnerability?"

Hunter snapped at her suddenly. "I'm sorry," he said immediately. "But why do you have to be so goddamned accurate all the time? Can I just work through this on my own terms?"

She was silent, and he knew from her silence that he'd hurt her feelings once again. But dammit, did she need to be so apt at reading him? Couldn't he, just for once in this life, feel like there was not someone standing there with their eyes trained on him trying to lead him through life's little disasters? Sightlings never got that kind of shit. Why did he?

"You know what? You're an asshole," Margie hissed.

"I know. I'm sorry."

"No, you don't know," Margie snapped, a small choke in her voice. "You think you know, but you don't because you're too fucking busy trying to be on the lookout for someone like your mother. And you still think nobody has ever had it as bad as poor Hunter, the little blind kid whose mommy didn't want to let him go. Well, fuck you."

"I said I'm sorry. Come on, Margie," he begged as she packed her stuff up and left with a slam of the door. "Fuck."

"Um, you still want me to read this script?" a voice came over the intercom.

Great. He drew a long breath as he reached for the switchboard Margie had abandoned. The mic had been open the whole time. Now the whole fucking studio knew he had a male escort for a potential heartthrob and not enough goddamn sense to just let it be sex. He gave a small, tight sigh. Had his own discomfort with Dillon's background come to this already? "No, I'm going to have to reschedule. Sorry. Margie will be in touch with you again at a later date. Could you let anyone else out there know that as well?" he asked.

"Sure."

He flipped the switch and closed himself off to the rest of the world. Despite the bravado, that was exactly how he felt at the moment, at most moments really. And now what was he supposed to do? Margie was pissed, which meant they wouldn't get any work done and Dillon… What was he supposed to do there? Just wait around until he decided to show up again? Was that how this was going to work? "You're such an idiot," he whispered to himself.

Maybe Margie was right. Maybe the plant was just part of the game.

Chapter 8

When Dillon was eleven years old, his father pulled out plans for a boat. He and his own father had built one together and he wanted to share a similar experience with Dillon. The difference, he told Dillon, was that his father had bought a kit, but this time he and Dillon would do it from scratch. It was going to be the plans, the elbow grease, and the wood. No kits. Dillon's mother had laughed, jokingly wondering who would dare voyage in such a craft, but his father had only flashed a look of unadorned injury at her before he winked at Dillon in quiet conspiracy.

They spent hundreds of hours out in the barn working together in the cool of the night. It was too hot during the day in the summer months so he and his father would sneak off after supper with a light chiding from his mother. Then they'd spend the late hours laughing while wood chips flew and the crickets chirped outside in the fields. In the winter, they'd slip in cocoa and coffee. Eventually, a wood stove was put in so they could spend more than an hour outside without his mother fussing at them about catching colds.

When they finished two and a half years later, they proudly launched it into a nearby lake and christened it, The Abigail, after his mother. She laughed and joked about it at the launching party, but she'd been very proud. She never believed they'd get it finished, or that it might actually float. But it did. And just as Dillon was starting puberty, they began their weekend excursions out on the lake. Just him, his dad, the fish, and the boat they'd built with their own hands.

But Dillon had a secret by that time. He'd been plagued with daydreams of kissing boys under the sweet gum trees in the back yard. He prayed his parents would be…not quite accepting, but at least minimally tolerant. He knew their complete approval was impossible even then, but he never fathomed the level of revulsion he'd experience in later years. He dreamed of love and a relationship, and of someone he could care about who would love him back.

When he was sixteen, part of his dream came true. Michael, a boy he knew from church, kissed him under one of those trees for his birthday. The kiss developed into much more.

But Michael was naïve and immature. Dillon didn't realize how naïve until weeks later, when Michael kissed him again in front of the whole congregation, as if nobody would notice him leaning over the pew to give him a quick peck on the cheek.

It was so innocent but so thoughtless among those people so chiseled in their angry religious hatred. Michael wasn't stupid. Dillon understood that. Michael was just one of those souls who only saw the joy in things and not the harshness which surrounded them.

The pastor didn't see it as innocent. He started yelling about demons in their midst and Dillon knew, right then, that life as he knew it was over.

Dillon's father was a pillar of the community. He would not

have a queer son. But he didn't yell. He didn't say a thing, not a single word. He simply turned and walked out of the church, expecting Dillon and his mother to follow. His neck was so swollen with a silent red rage that Dillon thought his head would pop off.

The last Dillon saw of Michael, he was being hustled out the door. His father was holding him by one arm and shouting homophobic slurs as he swatted at Michael's head.

In the final week after that kiss, Dillon didn't sleep and didn't eat. He barely showered. Most of the time, he sat in his room and stared at the wall waiting and hoping his father would come and talk to him instead of staring at the floor as they passed. Dillon tried speaking to him twice, but his dad had walked away, the disgust on his face plainly visible.

One night, he overheard his parents talking about how it may have been Michael who had turned Dillon gay, but they both knew it was a lie before his father even finished the sentence. Dillon wanted to rush into their room and tell them that it wasn't true. He was still the same person he'd always been. But he chickened out and crept back to his bedroom, afraid to say anything that would make the situation worse than it already was.

The next morning, Dillon's father took the boat out to the lake and burned it to the waterline. He stayed and watched the flames until it finally sank. He wouldn't look at Dillon when he came back with the empty trailer and flatly refused to sit at the same table with him any longer. It was Dillon's mother who finally suggested Dillon leave. She told him he'd broken his father's heart and only God would be able to help him.

He remembered screaming at her, screaming and running to the locked door of his parents' bedroom and beating on it as he begged his father to speak to him. By the time he'd wrung himself dry, his mother had packed his clothes and left them in a suitcase by the door.

No more words were spoken. When Dillon finally asked her where he should go, her only reply was that he should've considered that before becoming an abomination in the eyes of God.

Devastated, Dillon skulked to his cousin's house after sitting in the woods for a few hours. He didn't know what else to do, or where else to go. Travis hadn't been in the church on Sunday, but Dillon had no doubt whatsoever that Travis knew what happened.

Hell, everyone knew about it, the whole fucking town. In fact, he was pretty sure Travis already knew he was being tossed into the street. Such were the relations between his mom and aunt.

All the way there, through every field, he wondered what he'd say. When he got there, he paused before slipping in the back door, suddenly afraid of the revulsion he might find in his blind cousin's face.

Travis tilted his head up when Dillon stepped silently into his room and shut the door. He listened to Dillon's labored breath just as he'd done a thousand times before in his short, sightless life. "So they did it?" Travis asked.

"You know?" Dillon heard all he needed to know in Travis' question. His dismissal had been planned and orchestrated.

Travis nodded. "They asked me all kinds of weird shit – if you ever molested me, that sort of thing." He was quiet for a moment, listening to the sudden angry intake of Dillon's breath. They had been close as kids even though Dillon was two years older. Most people thought they were brothers. Dillon watched out for him and they spent almost every moment at one or the other's house.

He and Travis had messed around when they were very young, as any close boys would, but Dillon never thought of Travis as a sexual partner as he matured and realized his own interests. Not that he hadn't been curious, but it was just too gross, and to think his parents had asked something like that… "What did you tell them?" Dillon demanded.

"The fuck you think? Give me a break," Travis retorted as he sat there, a sudden shyness developing between them that had never existed before. "Why didn't you tell me?" he asked Dillon suddenly, seeming angry about it.

"Did I have to? Would it have made any difference?" Dillon barked in return.

"No, and that's why you should have told me," Travis answered immediately. "I don't give a shit."

They could have had a long discussion about how many times the words got to the very edge of Dillon's lips only to get stuck behind his teeth. They bit into him, bleeding a fear that Travis would react like his parents had. Dillon had been worried that he'd go all bible-thumper and tell all his friends. But none of that happened because Dillon had never been able to summon the courage to speak the words.

"What are you going to do?" Travis asked.

Tears started forming, tears which Travis couldn't see but which he'd catch in the gnawing ache of Dillon's voice. "I don't know. I don't have any place to go."

"You can't stay here. My dad will shoot you." Travis told him.

It was like his whole life was summed up at that moment. His parents had been bad, but this…this. "Okay," he finally whispered, choking on everything the word encompassed and held back.

The chair creaked as Travis stood and held his arms out. Dillon rushed to him and snatched his younger cousin into his arms. They squeezed each other; no words were adequate or necessary.

"Don't forget me," Travis whispered.

"Never." He leaned down and nuzzled Travis' temple, pulling in his scent and all the frolicking memories of the days and nights they had spent with each other in boyish bliss. All of it a blueprint about the type of effortless beauty Dillon had always wanted in his life. "Never," he whispered again.

They pulled apart, their arms awkward appendages hanging at their sides. "I better go," Dillon said.

"Here, wait." Travis reached into his desk, pulled out a can, and took out a wad of crumpled bills. "Take this and get the bus to Atlanta."

"Why?" Dillon asked. "Why Atlanta?"

"Easier to survive in the city," Travis told him. "Easier to hide."

"They won't come looking," Dillon answered as he took the money and stuffed it into his pocket.

"No," Travis shook his head, "but I might."

"They'd put you away," Dillon said. And they both knew it was true. Travis' father was a radical warrior for his God and they'd had more than a few conversations about how large the growing divide was between Travis and his dad. If Travis even thought about leaving, he'd be labeled a delinquent and hustled off to juvenile hall or some Christian youth rehab hell-hole.

"Exactly," Travis said. "But you're still going to have to get by and you won't be able to do that around here."

Dillon nodded at the sense of it and grabbed Travis' shoulder, squeezing it as he spoke. Nothing had ever come between them – not friends, not other family members, not school or sports or any of the ten million boy things that break up small friendships. "You're right. I should've told you. I'm sorry."

Travis smiled. "No sweat. I always knew you were a fag anyway," he added and laughed.

Dillon swatted at him and laughed. "Suck it."

They became quiet again as the seriousness of the situation came back to them.

"You have a backpack I can borrow?" Dillon asked. "My mom put my shit in a suitcase. I can't carry that around."

Travis grabbed his bag from the chair and dumped it on his bed, handing it to Dillon after he'd checked all the small pockets.

Dillon repacked it with his stuff and stood looking at Travis when he was done. "I better go. Thanks for the money." They shook, Dillon giving him another tap on the shoulder before he climbed out of the window.

"Atlanta," he said to himself as he repositioned the backpack and started walking through the fields to the bus station. He looked back over his shoulder and saw Travis sitting at his desk. He was looking out a window he couldn't see, and into a night which was as black as his vision. It was the last time Dillon saw him.

***

Ten years later, the words Dillon's mother spoke still clung to him. They were a wound that never healed. Even after a decade, the scab was still ripe and fresh and sometimes, like now, he scratched at it. Most of the time, he tried to ignore it.

Forget it he could not do, ever. And he had no misconceptions about that. He'd loved his father deeply, still loved him. But no matter how many times he considered it, he could not reconcile the gentle man who raised him with the indifferent bastard who had turned his back and allowed his wife to toss their only child from the house at the age of sixteen.

Would he ever be able to share that with someone like Hunter – someone normal who had loving parents and a place he called home? Would he want to? A rotten apple didn't fall far from the tree, or so the perception was here in the Deep South. What kind of revulsion might he witness in Hunter's face after hearing such a tale and all he did to survive afterward?

Chapter 9

It had been nine days since Hunter's argument with Margie in the studio. She'd been her usually efficient self as far as the business was concerned, but she'd rejected Hunter's many attempts at apologizing. She would just click off when their business was finished and not pick up after.

With Dillon coming around, Margie's friendship seemed less pressing than their professional relationship. It was strained, but it worked. Unfortunately, Hunter had gotten worried to the point that he kept expecting a call about Margie having found another job. He wasn't about to let that happen.

Besides the fact that Margie was his right hand and got a percentage of each sale, she was also a real friend. Hunter didn't want to lose that friendship. He had too few to sacrifice. As a blind gay man, his circle of friends was severely limited as was his ability to meet new people. Nightclubs were out. All the noise, plus the fact that he couldn't tell who was with who, or who might be interested in him. And never mind trying to navigate through the place. He'd attempted that once and it had been more than enough.

For most other gay men, he was a curiosity – a novelty they could show off to their friends. Look at my blind date, aren't I so socially forward? He'd come close to slapping one guy who tried to show Hunter off while they were out for dinner with a group of his friends.

Then there were the drama queens and the perfectionists who wouldn't even consider him for friendship, much less dating. Those queers who were so insecure about their looks that they needed someone who could constantly reassure them about their visual appeal were out, as were those who saw his disability as an infringement on their future. It wasn't hard to understand why he'd stayed single and thrown himself into his work. Dating just wasn't worth all the hassles that came with it, especially as a blind man.

And now there was Dillon. He wanted Dillon, and as more than just a fuck buddy. But he was still brooding about it, and that brooding had led him to lash out at his only real friend.

He picked up the phone and pressed the autodial for Margie again. She probably wouldn't answer, but he was going to try again anyway. Maybe complete and honest humility would help.

"It's Hunter," he said when the service picked up. "Listen, I know you're there, so just listen for a second. I know I'm a piece of shit, and you were completely right about Dillon. But…I need your help. I really like this guy. I can't explain it any better than that. You were right. I did fall for him and…well, I'm kind of hoping he's fallen for me too. I know how lame this sounds over the phone…" He stopped and rubbed his forehead as he tried to put his emotions into words. "Fuck, I don't know. I want you to meet him and tell me what you think. Anyway, call me back, please."

He put the phone down hoping it would ring right back. It didn't. She didn't return his call until he was getting ready to jump in the shower a few hours later.

"Speak," she commanded.

"I'm sorry, Margie. I really am. I'm an insensitive dickhead and I'd like to be able to blame it on someone else, but that's all me."

"Keep going."

"What else do you want me to say? I'm sorry. I've never meant to come across as the twat I was the other day. You know you're my bestie. It's just…this guy has my head so fucked up. I don't know which way to turn."

She was quiet for a moment. "Have you been out on a real date with him yet?" Margie asked.

"No, not yet."

"You should go out with him first. You've known him what, a couple of weeks? Spend some time together that's not between the sheets. See what he's really like. Then I'll meet him."

"You could come with us," Hunter offered.

"A third wheel on the first date. No, thanks."

"Okay, I'll do it. How about we set up lunch then, the three of us? Maybe on a Friday? You can check him out and call me back later. That way it's not so formal."

"After your first date," Margie reiterated.

"After my first date, yes. Deal?"

"Deal."

"Good," Hunter answered, relief flooding through him. "And you are my bestie, Margie, even if I've never said that before."

She clicked off. She wasn't going to let him off that easy.

Chapter 10

Having a face to face with Roland was a rare occurrence but not unheard of. In their seven-year partnership, Dillon had sat down with Roland twice, and both times had been enough to make him realize the man had probably saved his life. The first time he'd asked for a job in Roland's escort service, and the second time they talked about a client who turned into a stalker. Both times Dillon had been anxious, but not near as nervous as he was now.

Roland was thick and dark with a build which warned of his strength. What his size hid was how fast he was, and how furious he became when his business was threatened. He fronted as an insurance agency. He actually did sell insurance, but his investment clients, as they were referred to, were the bulk of his business and the core around which he'd built his elite customer base.

That was how he and Dillon met.

***

One of Roland's escorts, Jeremy, found Dillon behind his condo propped up against a dumpster. Dillon was dressed only in his boxers and completely oblivious as to where he was or how he got there. It was the second time in his life he'd been found behind a dumpster.

At first, Jeremy thought Dillon was dead and had freaked out, screaming until Dillon groaned. Once he realized Dillon was still alive, Jeremy called Roland and brought Dillon to his condo, handing him a pair of sweats and a cup of coffee while they waited.

Roland arrived within the hour looking for answers. A few weeks prior, one of his other escorts ended up in the same predicament and Roland had put the word out. He expected his boys to report anything similar or suspicious. Nobody messed with his business and he wanted payback.

At first, Dillon thought that he was just another pimp protecting his interests. He'd seen plenty of them in three years on the street and had been approached by several. But watching Roland calm the still flustered Jeremy, and witnessing his attentiveness firsthand, gave Dillon a different picture of the man. Later, he learned that none of Roland's escorts walked the streets.

Roland had an elite client list whose needs were discretely catered to for large sums of money. Fuck boys, drama queens, meth heads never made it anywhere near Roland's clients.

After the incident, Dillon and Jeremy became friends and through that friendship, a professional relationship developed with Roland. Dillon didn't realize it then, but Roland started checking into him and had Jeremy keeping tabs. Some months later, when Jeremy suggested that maybe Dillon might want to contact Roland and get out of street hustling, it had been at Roland's prompting.

The escort service was a dream for Dillon. Since Roland's escorts were listed as insurance salesmen, they pulled a paycheck, paid taxes, and never handled cash. Roland managed everything behind the scenes before the service was even brokered. Any tips they made were theirs to keep, and Roland would often slide them a bonus when a client made an exceptional comment. Dillon had received several of those.

But Roland was no pushover. One major client complaint, one mishap with drugs, one step outside his customer base, and you were done. His clients paid for exclusivity and that's what he gave them. Dillon didn't think Roland ever hurt anyone himself, but he was aware of three escorts who had crossed Roland and who were not seen in the city again.

And as for the guy who had drugged and beat him and Roland's other escort, Roland made sure to slide Dillon a picture when he gave Dillon his first check. It wasn't pretty.

***

All this history raced through Dillon's mind as he came in and stood in the middle of the room waiting for Roland to look up.

He'd finally made the decision to leave the business. He still didn't know how he was going to talk to Hunter about it, but the decision was made. Hunter had made him understand that he could find a life outside of hustling. He wanted Hunter in that life, but there was still so much wrapped up inside of him that Hunter didn't know about. He was afraid of what Hunter would think if he just came right out and told him he'd quit the business. He let those concerns go for a moment.

Worrying about what would happen later wasn't getting it done. First, he had to break it to Roland and then he'd figure out how to talk to Hunter. He had to figure out how to tell him how he really felt without scaring him off.

He took a breath and looked around. Roland's office never changed. It had a tropical picture calendar for a decoration behind the desk and four nondescript prints on the other walls which looked like they came out of the last century. One wooden chair sat directly in front of Roland's expansive desk. The room was barren, pointless, and every vice cop's worst nightmare, just as Roland intended it to be.

"Are you going to sit?" Roland asked without looking up from what he was doing.

Dillon sat quietly. He rubbed his hands on his pants and realized he was shaking slightly. When it came right down to it, he'd broken the house rules. He'd propositioned Hunter on the street like a common crack whore, had unprotected sex, and he'd failed to give Hunter the central business number used to make appointments. These were all reasons for instant dismissal.

"Well?" Roland asked, his focus still on his work.

Dillon took a breath. "I've met someone." He'd not only met him, but he'd also given the money back and he'd gone back to Hunter's apartment several times since. Each time it became a sexual carnival that pressed more against his chest than it did his groin. But none of that came out of his mouth.

Roland glanced up at him and rolled his eyes before he went back to the paperwork on his desk. "And? I never said you couldn't have a personal life. You know that."

Roland glanced up a second time, appraising Dillon's

continued silence. He put his pen down and gave Dillon his full attention. "Let me guess, he wants to take you away. He's going to fill your ass with promises and sunshine so you won't have to hustle anymore," Roland said as he pushed the paperwork aside, folded his hands on his desk, and cocked his head.

Dillon's concerns eased a little. It seemed obvious Roland knew the reason for his visit. "Come on, don't you think I've been in the game long enough not to fall for that kind of bullshit? Don't I get any credit?" Dillon asked.

Roland grunted and studied Dillon for a long moment. "So what's the deal? If this isn't about some sugar daddy coming to the rescue, then what is it? You've got such an easy client base, why would you want to give that up? It's like free money. And who else is going to take care of the geriatrics like you do?"

Dillon smirked. Because of the status and wealth of most of Roland's client base, Dillon's customers tended to be more mature than the average john. In the last two years, every time a new client above the age of sixty called, Roland had tried to pawn them off on Dillon.

Dillon wasn't sure why, but he'd never complained. They were easy clients, not overly sexual and typically very pleasant men. All but one had been prominent Southern gentlemen who were very secure in their status and not afraid of being generous. "I'm sure you'll find someone," he told Roland. "And I'll visit and talk to my regulars before I go."

"They'll probably throw you a fucking party and start giving you going away gifts," Roland chuckled. "But you didn't answer my question."

Dillon shrugged, his anxiety returning. "I've got to find something for myself. I'm getting too old for this shit." He looked down at his hands, wringing them around each other like he was a child in the principal's office. "And too lonely," he added quietly.

"Oh Christ, don't be getting all maudlin on me. Just go do what you got to do. If it doesn't work out, you can always come back here. You know that," Roland said, shuffling the papers on his desk again.

Dillon's eyes darted back to his face. "You're not mad?"

Roland shrugged, leaned back in his chair, and looked up at the ceiling. "What would I be angry about? You got all that money from Shawn, right?" he asked pointedly, glancing at Dillon.

Fear etched its way back into Dillon's face.

Roland cocked an eyebrow and sat forward again. "It's your money. Stop looking like I'm going to eat your face off. It's my job to know what's going on with you guys. Did you really think I didn't know?" He leaned back again. "I've been expecting this conversation. That kind of thing doesn't happen too often, but I'm glad it was you."

Dillon stared at him, utterly astonished at the idea that another escort had been left a shitload of money by a client. "You know someone else?"

"Me," Roland answered. "How do you think I built this business?" he asked waving his hand around. "But that was a long time ago, and entirely different circumstances."

Dillon watched him for a moment. Roland had never shared anything personal. It was always strictly business. "I think that's the nicest thing you've ever said to me. I feel all special and tingly," Dillon teased him.

"Get the fuck outta here. Go chase this man you found."

"I…"

Roland held his hand up. "Yeah, whatever. Save that shit for someone who hasn't been around the block. It's written all over you plain as day. This conversation doesn't have anything to do with Shawn's money or you tricking, and we both know it. Find him, love him, and make sure he loves you back before you throw everything away. Now get," he said, pointing a thick finger at the door.

Dillon smiled before he got up and turned for the door. Whatever he might say or do, Roland had a soft spot in his heart and always did, even when it came to busting heads that was sometimes necessary for this line of work. Dillon was going to miss the man; there was no doubt about it. When he'd had no home to go to, Roland had helped him make one. No one else did.

"Dillon?"

He looked back at Roland.

"Don't start an escort service," Roland suggested with a stern glance.

Dillon laughed. "No need to worry about that."

Roland nodded and smiled. "Good. Keep in touch, huh?"

Dillon nodded back, closed the door behind him, and walked

out to his car. The night was quiet but still chilly. Now all he had to do was figure out if Hunter wanted him in his life or if what they had was just about sex. It was pretty easy to take Hunter's casual statements and warp them into a dream, but Dillon had to ask himself if Hunter was ready to lay claim to a former prostitute. He wasn't too sure he'd do it himself, so he had no illusions about Hunter's potential concerns.

And then Dillon had his family to consider. He didn't know how he intended to deal with those issues. He'd been excellent at suppressing his feelings about them over the years. But that was easy to do when you only spent a few hours with a trick and didn't interact with them on a day to day basis.

What would Hunter do when Dillon fell into one of his inexplicable funks? What would he say when he learned that Dillon had sucked dick for a ten spot just so he could eat for the first three years?

Now that he was a successful whore everything seemed rosy, but what would happen when Hunter knew his roots? What then? He had no skills, no real education, and not a goddamned thing going for him except his looks and his new money. Neither of which were worth a damn when it actually came down to it. Hunter couldn't see what he looked like and it didn't seem as if he needed Dillon's money.

He shook his head. How the hell was he going to convince Hunter of their potential when he couldn't even see it himself?

Chapter 11

It took Dillon a few days to sort out his affairs and dredge up the courage to return to Hunter's apartment. He stood downstairs staring at the call box worried that he was showing up unannounced too often.

Maybe Hunter was tired of him already. Maybe he had other plans or other men. Dillon really didn't know a damned thing about Hunter except he was blind and great in bed. And it wasn't like he called beforehand. He was just plain stupid for this guy and he didn't even have his phone number. How ridiculous was that?

He'd made all these grand plans in his head and didn't even have the basics covered. But Jesus, he just felt like he needed to be near this guy. It felt so…right. He drew a breath and pressed the buzzer.

"Yes?" Hunter answered.

"It's me."

"Oh, I was just thinking about you. Come up."

Well, that was a good sign. He bounced up the stairs and saw Hunter waiting with the door open.

"Do you remember the new bistro you saw over on Tenth Street?" Hunter asked as soon he approached.

"Um…"

"The one with the soaped over windows," Hunter prodded,

trying to refresh his memory. "I asked you to describe our surroundings the day you picked me up."

"Oh yeah, I remember," Dillon answered, noting Hunter's choice of words. It wasn't the day they'd met. It was the day Dillon picked him up. He looked down at his shoes and wondered if he should've come up.

"Would you like to go?" Hunter asked.

Dillon studied him. Hunter seemed excited, bouncing on his feet like some little kid. Maybe he was overplaying his fears again. He had such a bad habit of doing that since he'd hit the streets. "Like on a date? In public?" he asked, teasing Hunter to mask his insecurity. "And here I thought you might be letting me hang out just for the sex."

Hunter's fingers followed Dillon's voice. They traced their way up the front of Dillon's shirt and slipped around to cup his neck as he leaned into him. "On second thought…"

"Uh-uh," Dillon said, stepping away. "You're not getting out of dinner. When would you like to go? We could go right now, it's not too late." The idea of a real date sounded like a great first step. It would give him the opportunity to find out if Hunter actually wanted him as much as he wanted Hunter.

"Tomorrow?" Hunter asked.

"Okay. I'll swing by on my way home and see if they're open yet."

"But you don't have to leave right now, do you?" Hunter asked. He threaded his fingers behind Dillon's belt and yanked him closer, pressing their lips together. "Unless, of course, you have to go somewhere," he added as he slid his hand down the front of Dillon's pants.

Dillon stared at his mouth, the curve of his lips. "No, nowhere," he answered in a husky whisper, the texture of his words matching Hunter's fervor. He grabbed Hunter's waist and pulled him close.

"Mm," Hunter moaned as he stroked Dillon to hardness. "You just don't know how much I like these surprise visits."

***

The soapy windows had disappeared. Inside the bistro, they found a bustling establishment owned and staffed almost exclusively by gay men. The food was simple but excellent, an Italian-French fusion which brought in all the flavors of the Mediterranean. It smelled magnificent as soon as they walked in — garlic and herbs and fresh bread wafting its yeasty aroma from somewhere. When they sat down, the waiter poured fresh olive oil in a small dish which resonated with a fruity bouquet.

Hunter made a mental note to learn the full extent of the menu and their willingness to deliver. Of all the skills he'd learned at the school for the blind, cooking had never been his strong point. Besides the mess, he couldn't cook worth a damn and preferred to use the microwave if given the choice.

"You know, I think I'm starting to like your friend," Dillon commented after he'd ordered a bottle of wine.

"Margie?"

"Is she the one who made you walk home?"

Hunter laughed. "She didn't make me. I told her to stop the car or I was going to jump out of the damned thing."

"I thought she demanded this dinner."

"I make her sound like a real bitch, don't I?" Hunter chuckled. "I wanted you to meet her, but she didn't want to be a third wheel. She thought we needed a chance to get to know each other better."

"Rather than just fuck?"

Hunter burst out laughing. "Yeah, such an absurd woman." He got serious. "She is my bestie, though, and I've treated her like shit lately."

"I'll have to thank her when we meet. Maybe I'll tell her to make some more demands. I kind of like this one."

Hunter blushed. Why was it that even the vaguest compliment from Dillon made him feel like he was that frisky thirteen-year-old blind kid accidentally bumping into his friends and copping clandestine touches at the same time? "She'd like to have lunch. I can introduce you properly then," he told Dillon.

"Just give me the where and when and I'm there."

Their waiter came over and they went through the menu with Dillon inserting questions about the food and their fusion style. Hunter ordered with Dillon's suggestions and they settled back to nibble on the fresh bread the waiter brought to the table.

Hunter smiled. This was so different from the Rat Hole he almost laughed out loud just thinking about it. "So now that we've been forced on this date, what's your deep burning question? What do you want to know about me?"

Dillon paused for a moment. "Who do you envy?" he asked.

"That's an odd question."

"It is," Dillon acknowledged. "I heard a shrink claim it was a good indicator of character and neurosis."

Hunter considered his answer before he spoke. "I'd have to say, people who are a total spazz, you know what I mean? I was raised to believe everything had to be proper. You live, grow old, die and never really say what's on your mind. To me, it felt like listening to music without being able to groove." He did a little wiggle in his chair which made Dillon smirk. "It's very straight laced and boring; very Southern. There's no joy in that. So, in all honesty, I'd have to say those people who are the what-the-fuck types. I like them even though I'm still trapped in my proper Southern upbringing. I envy their freedom."

"I like that," Dillon told him.

"Who do you envy?" Hunter asked him in return.

"Ah, no fair. You have to come up with your own profoundly, snooty question," Dillon replied, mentally avoiding all the small desires that had grown inside him over the years. "But if I were pushed, I'd have to say you and your hot body."

Hunter blushed again and laughed. "Yeah, okay." He cocked his head to the side, nibbling on a piece of bread. "When did you figure out you were gay?"

"That's not profound or snooty," Dillon informed him.

"No, but I'm interested," Hunter remarked. For him, that period of his life had been different than he assumed it was for most kids. He didn't get the visual cues and the who-looks-hot updates, nor could he see what a new hairstyle did for someone. Instead, he got scents and smells, and rarely some exploratory touches which he sometimes instigated. But he understood early on that he was attracted to boys.

He also ran into what his mother called the cute blind boy problem before he informed her he was gay. The girls he went to school with, and those sighted girls in church and town, all wanted him as a boyfriend. For some reason, they held to a bizarre and false security that Hunter's blindness somehow meant that he was safe from wanting to fuck their brains out. He could never figure it out. He was just as horny as any other teenage boy. Just because he was blind, didn't mean his dick didn't get hard when the wind blew. Had he been straight well…they might have run into some serious problems.

"Mm, about eleven or so, I guess," Dillon answered his question. "I didn't use gay, of course. I didn't know what that was. But I knew I liked boys. Never actually acted on it until I hit puberty and then I kept catching the wood when I thought about my classmates. And if you want me to be really honest, I always wondered what it would be like with my cousin too. I mean we messed around when we were really small, but kids' stuff. Show me yours, I'll show you mine kind of thing."

"Your cousin?" Hunter asked.

"My blind cousin and my best friend back then."

"You little perv," Hunter joked. Not missing the fact that Dillon's inflection had altered to something much more guarded when the conversation touched on his family.

"Yeah," Dillon murmured, a smile blooming in his voice. "I was that. Still am."

"So the day you picked me up you were chasing an old pubescent fantasy about getting into your cousin's pants?" Hunter asked.

Dillon laughed. "No." He hesitated. "I don't know…it was…with him I never had to prove anything. My sexuality, my looks, they just didn't make a difference one way or another. I didn't have to fake it with him. I could just be myself. And we were never sexual. He didn't even know until the end. Maybe I was looking to grab at some of that realism again," Dillon surmised.

To Hunter, it sounded as if he were trying to evaluate his actions the day he'd propositioned him.

"He was the realest person I ever knew," Dillon continued. "Honestly, I'm not sure what made me ask you. But I knew I couldn't ignore that ass walking down the street, cane or no cane," he said and started laughing as Hunter bloomed a bright red across the table.

Their food came out and they oo-ed and ah-ed when the manager came over and asked how everything was.

**

As dinner continued, Dillon realized what it was that made

him want to be with Hunter. It wasn't just his body. Hunter wasn't in the dark. Even though he was blind, he saw more than most people ever did. He didn't allow his handicap or people's expectations of his disability to limit him, and that kept pulling Dillon back to him. He exuded confidence and emitted an innate understanding that there were so many more people so much blinder than he. And, he really didn't seem to give a shit what other people thought. But there was more, and even though he couldn't quite touch on it right at that moment, he intended to find out what it was.

Dinner came to an end, as did their quiet conversation. They had walked over from Hunter's apartment because it was so close and the night was quiet and warmer than the last few days had been. Winter was coming and they realized that soon they'd have to drive if they wanted to come back again, which they'd both agreed would be necessary.

Dillon walked beside Hunter on their return to his apartment, his hand resting gently in the crook of Hunter's arm. "That was nice. Our first real date," he said, quietly hoping there would be many more to follow.

"I think that was Margie's intent." Hunter smiled and turned his head to the sound of Dillon's voice. "Does this mean we can go home and fuck now, or should I call Margie and check if that's okay?"

Dillon burst out laughing. "We might be able to arrange that."

"Just kidding," Hunter said. "Well, not completely. But thank you, I really enjoyed dinner." He paused for a moment. "I thought we could do lunch with Margie this Friday if you don't have anything planned."

Before Dillon could respond, a man slipped from the shadows and stuck the point of a knife in Hunter's back. "Give me your fucking money, faggots," he said from behind Hunter. He'd turned and placed Hunter between himself and Dillon, thinking Dillon was more of a threat to him than Hunter was. He took a grip on Hunter's neck, holding him in place while he lifted his knife momentarily and waved it at Dillon for emphasis. "Now."

"Whoa, chill. You can have it," Dillon said as he reached for his wallet. "We don't want any trouble."

"Fuck that!" Hunter spat. He slid his walking cane into his hand and slammed the top of it backward into the man's solar plexus. He spun, gripping his cane from the end and took the guy's feet out from underneath him while he was bent double and still gasping for breath. He heard the knife go clanging off on the pavement somewhere.

Hunter moved in instantly. He outlined the mugger's body with his cane to give him an idea of his position and began striking him with sharp blows that were meant to let the asshole know who he'd picked for a target. Hunter wouldn't hurt him too bad, but the guy wouldn't forget him anytime soon either.

"Jesus Christ!" Dillon blurted. It had taken Hunter less than two minutes to disarm and subdue their attacker. Dillon stood utterly dumbfounded while the man groaned at Hunter's feet.

"Where's the knife?" Hunter snapped at him, knowing that the situation could change back just as quickly as it had begun.

Dillon reached down and picked it up, slipping it into his pocket as he stood. "I've got it."

"Is there anyone else around?" Hunter asked. "His friends?"

"No," Dillon replied, looking around before he answered. "We're alone."

"Good." Hunter brought his cane squarely down on the guy's nuts and listened to him moan again. "That should hold him for a while."

He straightened from his stance and slid his hands up and down his cane until he found the notch he was looking for. He placed the red-tipped end on the ground and started walking home as if nothing happened.

"Where the fuck did you learn that?" Dillon exclaimed, stepping up beside Hunter as he glanced back and checked at their would-be assailant one more time. "I thought that thing was aluminum," he said of Hunter's walking stick.

"No, Sitka spruce. It's what they make guitars and stringed instruments from," Hunter told him. "It's light but unyielding. I had it made special for me. It's called a Jo, or a short staff; the only weapon ever to defeat master swordsman Miyamoto Musashi." He stopped and handed it to Dillon. "Here, feel."

Dillon took it from him and hefted its light weight before handing it back. He glanced back at the mugger and saw that he'd crawled to his feet and was hobbling in the opposite direction.

He started laughing and kept laughing until he had to stop and lean against a wall to catch his breath.

"What?" Hunter asked.

"That was the funniest shit I have ever seen," Dillon said and started laughing again. "You just stomped his ass, Hunter. We could have put that on YouTube."

Hunter smiled and then shrugged. He'd continued his martial arts training specifically so he wouldn't feel like a perpetual victim.

"Where'd you learn that?" Dillon asked again as he straightened up and fell in beside Hunter.

"I take private lessons at a dojo in Dunwoody. It's right off the Marta so I can hop on at Tenth and get off there," Hunter answered.

"That was so awesome. You're like all kung fu and shit," Dillon said and started chuckling again. "I kind of feel sorry for that poor bastard. That last one must have hurt."

"I don't," Hunter said. "He thought we were easy targets because I was blind and we were gay. I hope I fucking neutered him, piece of shit."

Dillon started laughing again then suddenly reached out, stopping himself just as he was about to grab Dillon's face. "Can I kiss you?" he asked quietly. "I don't want to end up on the ground with your stick in my ass. Well, not that one anyway."

Hunter smirked. "Here, in front of God and all these fine citizens? We'd be scandalized."

"Why not here?" Dillon asked as he moved in closer, his

voice getting low. "We're not having sex, yet."

Hunter moved forward slowly, brushing his lips against Dillon's with a light passion that didn't encompass the adrenaline still running through his system. He really wanted to grind into Dillon's lips but held himself back, relishing in their dampened ecstasy instead. He took a deep breath when Dillon stepped back, suddenly relaxed by Dillon's still tenderness.

"You're crying," Dillon said quietly. He thumbed away a tear. "What's wrong?"

Hunter wiped his face and brushed the tears away, embarrassed by them. "Nothing, just an adrenaline rush," he told Dillon. But even as he said it he knew how ridiculously untruthful that sounded. What he didn't want to say was how real he felt right at that moment. He'd just had a fantastic dinner, he had a beautiful man beside him, and he'd just overcome one of his worst fears as a blind man. All of it happening within the space of a few minutes.

He slid towards Dillon and felt his embrace as he kissed him again. He loved his strong arms and the passion he kept so tightly wrapped within himself. Were they really so different in that aspect?

It seemed they were always trying to hide their fears, always attempting to be the good Southern gentlemen they were raised to be. He wondered if they would ever move beyond that bullshit and just be completely honest with each other. Could they reach a place where they could just snuggle up and know, really know, that the other person understood all their darkest fears and was willing to sit right beside them and help fight those battles?

"Better?" Dillon asked as Hunter pulled away.

"Yes, thanks."

"Did I tell you how beautiful you are?" Dillon asked, still holding onto his hands.

"No, I don't think you did," Hunter said shyly. In fact, no one had ever said that to him before. Not once.

"Tsk, tsk. Obviously, you'll have to spank me for that failure later," Dillon told him with a gigantic grin in his voice.

Hunter smirked and started walking again. "You'd like that too much."

"You realize I have to come up with some kind of kung fu ninja name for you now, right?"

Hunter laughed. "Those are two entirely separate cultures."

"Whatever."

"As long as it's not Grasshopper, we'll be okay," Hunter told him. He felt Dillon's hand slip back into the crook of his arm.

"How did you know where to hit without seeing him?" Dillon asked curiously.

"His voice relative to yours gave me a general direction. His breath blowing on my neck gave me an approximate distance. Then his grip on my neck told me what his body position was. Thumbs will always give that away," Hunter told him as he wiggled his thumb in the air.

"All that?" Dillon asked. "You really are a ninja."

"Not really. You sightlings are so dependent on your vision that you miss a lot of other environmental cues," Hunter said. "My senses aren't any better than yours. I'm just tuned into the others more because I don't have vision clouding up the synapses."

"Sightlings?" Dillon laughed.

"Sorry, it's a derogatory term. We don't use that too often. It slipped out."

"Shu-shu would like you," Dillon said quietly.

"Shu-shu?" Hunter asked, hearing the tension that had been lingering in Dillon's voice suddenly drop off as soon as the words were out of his mouth. So much was hidden in him and it made Hunter wonder why.

"An old friend," Dillon answered vaguely. "You know, I've had sex with a blindfold on and, despite what people said, it never really did anything for me."

Hunter noted the subject change, but let it go. "Probably because you were too busy thinking about what you were missing with your eyes," Hunter remarked. "I think I have a mask at the house," he added with a quiet suggestion.

"You do?" Intrigue colored Dillon's voice.

Hunter stopped and reached out to touch Dillon's face. "We'll start right here. Keep your eyes closed," he said as he ran his fingers over Dillon's eyelids. "Now don't open them at all. I'll lead you back to the apartment. It's only around the corner. When we get there stay at the door and I'll bring the mask."

"This could get interesting."

"That's the plan," Hunter whispered leaning close to him. "Walking back without reference will help you adapt to a different level of perception. If you just slap a mask on two minutes before sex, your body hasn't adjusted, it's still focused on the lost sensory input."

"Like a mild form of panic," Dillon suggested.

"Yeah, I guess you could say that, but it's a little more subtle. Ready?" Hunter asked. He felt Dillon's grip tighten on him immediately. "Uh-uh, keep your grip loose. I'm not going to let you fall," Hunter reassured him.

Dillon's grip loosened, though it was still tighter than when he'd had his eyes open.

"Good, here we go. Just follow my lead," Hunter said as they started walking. It took them a few starts and stops as Dillon misstepped, but Hunter got him back to the apartment unharmed.

"Are your eyes still closed?" Hunter asked as he slid the key into the apartment door.

"Yes."

He brought Dillon inside and closed the door behind them. "Stay here. I want you to focus on the sound of my moving around. Listen as I walk away and come back, and don't turn on any lights," he instructed.

"It's already dark in here," Dillon said.

"Probably, but your inclination is to get a quick peek and try to reorient yourself. It's a subconscious reaction to a lack of stimuli," Hunter said. "Wait here."

Hunter went to the bedroom and dug through a small box at the back of the closet. A year or two before, he and Margie had stopped at a sex shop as a dare. He walked out with several hundred dollars' worth of kinky toys which he'd never used. One of the things Margie had insisted he needed was a mask. He'd argued that one blind person in the bedroom was enough, but now he was thankful for her persistence.

He pawed through the box and found the mask. It was still wrapped in cellophane, the price tag was dry and rough against his thumb as he ripped it open. "Hope this works," he muttered as he pushed the box back into the far reaches of the closet and got to his feet.

His cock started getting hard as he walked back to the front door. He rubbed himself through his pants in anticipation. This was going to be fun. "Eyes still closed?" he asked Dillon.

"Yes."

"I'm going to put this on you. It's supposed to offer a complete blackout, but I can't attest to that. Are you ready?"

He felt Dillon's hand tentatively reach up, find his cheek and caress the stubble on his jawline.

"Yes," Dillon answered with a rough ache.

Hunter smiled as he moved behind him and slipped the mask over his head. "You'll have to adjust it yourself. How does it feel?"

Dillon adjusted it. "Feels okay."

"Can you see anything?"

"Nothing."

"Good," Hunter whispered, sliding his arms around him from behind. "Are you listening?" Hunter asked at a barely audible level.

Dillon moaned as Hunter reached around and slowly massaged his cock through his pants. "Yes."

"I want you to focus on my touch and my breath, nothing else. Not my words, my breath. Okay?" Hunter asked him quietly.

"Yes."

"And no more talking." Hunter smiled, not sure if he wanted to fuck him by the front door or back in the bedroom. He had a hundred fantasies suddenly running through his head, but knew he could only pick one. He took his hand from Dillon's cock and slowly pulled his shirt up, allowing only the tips of his fingers to caress Dillon's skin while he worked the shirt over his head. His tongue traced down the back of Dillon's neck to the edge of his shoulder and retraced its path back up again, a slow metronome of moist heat.

Dillon's moan was expected and Hunter reached around and teased his nipples, brushing them to hardness before he pinched and pulled them slowly from Dillon's chest. It elicited a long, slow ache that Dillon echoed in his sigh.

He could feel Dillon trying to push his ass back against him, but he avoided the contact. Hunter wanted Dillon's body to beg for his touch without words. He wanted it to whisper its desire through the electricity his fingers would send as they made their way around the contours of Dillon's beauty. He sank his teeth into Dillon's neck, gently sucking as he purred against his skin. He knew the vibration would make Dillon just as hot as if he was mouthing those murmurs against the rigid veins in his cock.

He slid in front of Dillon and kept his fingertips skimming

Dillon's torso as he pushed him against the wall. Dillon's hands come up to embrace him, but he gently pushed them away and pressed them flat against the wall. Dillon would need them for support soon enough.

When Hunter's mouth found his nipple, Dillon gasped. It was a deep intake that made Hunter suck harder as if he were a child nursing on the teat. He pulled away and blew across it, hearing Dillon groan as the cold air rushed back and brought it to a higher level of sensation.

Hunter pressed further down, his tongue leaving a trail until he came to Dillon's belt. He reached up and tweaked Dillon's nipples one last time and rubbed his own chest against the heat Dillon's cock radiated through his dress pants.

He inhaled again, taking in Dillon's scent, swirling it in his nostrils and tasting it on his tongue. As he breathed, he could almost feel the elixir of Dillon's lust join the oils on his skin and reached to unfasten his pants. They fell straight to the floor leaving only Dillon's boxers as a defense against all the small tortures Hunter's tongue had devised.

Hunter blew on Dillon's cock once, took it into his mouth, and closed his lips around it, tasting the cotton now moist with pre-cum. He sucked the juices from the cotton and let it go while Dillon gasped above him, his hands in a tight grip against the wall.

He pulled back and went still, not moving or breathing, just letting Dillon feel the blank, black space around him; letting him wallow in confused disorientation and lustful curiosity. He could feel

Dillon's body heat against his face and smiled when he heard a small grunt of disappointment in Dillon's breath.

Hunter quickly took his shirt off then slipped out of the rest of his clothes, piling them beside the wall so he could find them later. Once he was undressed, he went back to Dillon, slipping his mouth around his still-sheathed cock and bringing it back to fullness with the warmth of his breath.

Reaching down, he untied Dillon's shoes and pulled off each one, caressing each foot as he lifted it from the floor. He inhaled the masculine sweat he found trapped between Dillon's toes and groaned. He couldn't help it. Above him, Dillon moaned as he took one socked foot and rubbed it on his face. He let Dillon's foot fall back to the floor and drew his slacks and boxers off until Dillon stood naked.

Dillon's cock was rigid, standing up straight against his abdomen. Hunter wanted to swallow it whole and work his tongue straight down to Dillon's balls while Dillon face-fucked him. But instead, he rubbed his lips and whiskers along its length and kissed Dillon's abdomen as he listened to the ragged, yearning gasps above him.

Hunter's breath was ragged. He was holding himself back. His small, clandestine touches had brought his own desire forward like a storm. He gnawed around the base of Dillon's cock and through his sparse, trimmed pubic hair. Above him, Dillon sucked in air in short, hard gasps.

Hunter ran his hands inside of Dillon's thighs, gently pushing them apart until Dillon got the hint and stepped to the side to give him greater access.

Hunter dropped to Dillon's feet again and began slowly licking his way up each of Dillon's legs. He was tasting the man in front of him as if he could taste every hair, every follicle, and every pore. When he finally got to Dillon's balls, he licked each of them before swallowing one in his mouth. He sucked on it as his hands slipped under Dillon's torso and found his anus.

God, he loved that hairless ass – the weight of it in his hands; the sharp definition of Dillon's cheeks, the musky aroma that was clean and sexual every time he got near it. He probed Dillon's hole delicately; slowing lubing him with the sweaty moisture that had started flowing down from Dillon's back.

Dillon gasped as soon as Hunter touched it; a hot fire in his breath that brought him up on his toes. But his hole wasn't begging yet. Only Dillon's breath was doing that. Hunter wanted to feel it grasp at his fingers and open and flex and try to pull them in before he turned Dillon around and stuck his tongue in their place.

He let Dillon's testicle slip from his mouth and pushed his lips against the base of Dillon's shaft again. He listened carefully as Dillon whimpered. His finger was rubbing Dillon's hole furiously as he worked his mouth to the head of Dillon's cock and took the whole of it deep into his throat.

He didn't close his mouth. He let his throat muscles work on Dillon's cock, massaging the head as he bobbed. When he felt Dillon's asshole open, he slammed his lips shut and took the length of him with his tongue. He forced Dillon's cock down his throat as he rammed his finger deep into Dillon's ass.

Dillon yelled in sudden and unexpected ecstasy, bringing his hands off the wall to grab at Hunter's head.

Hunter shook them off and pushed them back to the wall again. He slid down the length of Dillon's cock with his throat muscles in quick, hard, deep thrusts, countering Dillon's attempt at taking control.

He pulled away suddenly and sat back on his haunches, letting Dillon feel the sudden vacancy in his ass and the sudden loss of heat on his prick.

He almost laughed when Dillon let out a groan like a despairing little kid. He leaned forward and licked the very tip of Dillon's cock once more, tasting his pre-cum.

The man tasted so goddamned good.

He smiled again and grabbed Dillon by the hips. He turned Dillon to the wall and pushed his cheek and hands against it as he stood.

"Please?" Dillon whimpered, poking his ass out against Hunter's rock hard cock.

Hunter pressed the tip of his cock against Dillon's asshole and kissed the back of his neck. He groaned into Dillon's ear, rubbing his shaft along Dillon's sphincter without penetrating. He pulled away when Dillon tried to grab him and guide his cock in.

Hunter dropped to his knees. The hot flesh of Dillon's ass was before him, calling him. He licked it slowly, gently working his way across each globe as Dillon spread his stance further to offer him more. When he spread Dillon's cheeks, his tongue reached in like a hot dart. Dillon gasped.

Hunter lapped at Dillon's hole – licking and poking his tongue at it like it was an elixir. Dillon stretched upward on his toes again while he poked his ass back. His moans were a constant flurry of whimpers and protests that Hunter's tongue could only go so far.

It was a torment when Hunter stood. His hard cock rubbed against Dillon's asshole before he began a slow, slow entrance. He took Dillon deliberately; a cautious, careful, single movement which stretched Dillon's gasp into one long moan.

Dillon was beyond listening by then and Hunter knew it. All his focus was on tactile stimulation and he kept trying to push Hunter to go faster. Dillon wanted it harder, deeper. But Hunter wouldn't allow it.

He grinned as he brushed his lips across the back of Dillon's neck. He took Dillon's hips in his hands and pushed them away from him, drawing his cock out until just the head remained, building a slow momentum that kept increasing. He was very slow at first, letting Dillon feel his length, making him grasp each rigid vein with the muscles of his sphincter as he slid back in. In. Out. In again. Out again. So, so slow.

"Please," Dillon begged. He whimpered, his mewling a desperate craving. "Please." As soon as the word left his mouth, Dillon's body opened. His asshole flexed and invited Hunter in. It begged him to bury himself in hard, deep thrusts until he'd bred

Dillon and filled him with every ounce of cum his body could muster.

Hunter drew back and pulled himself completely out before he pushed Dillon flat against the wall and fucked him raw. He slammed into him, pistoning his cock into Dillon's ass until Dillon was on his toes a third time. Dillon's voice became a gyrating warble of ecstasy which filled the whole apartment until he came against the wall.

Hunter filled him as soon as he felt the grip of Dillon's sphincter tighten around his cock. He pushed in deep and let his body pump the seed into Dillon over and over and over again. His own breath coming in small gasps as he felt Dillon's body milking him for more. Wanting more. In a moment, he pulled out and heard the pop of his cock as Dillon slumped to the floor. He was still gasping.

Hunter turned Dillon's face to his softening cock and had him lick and clean it until he was satisfied that he could do no more. But even after he was done, Dillon was still breathless and whimpering for more. They hadn't even left the hallway yet.

Hunter smiled and stroked through the sweat in Dillon's hair. He reached down and gently coaxed Dillon to his feet. When he took his hand and led him to the bedroom, he thought Dillon might have gained a little understanding of what sex was like as a blind man. And now that they had both spent, the real fun could begin.

Dillon would soon learn what it was to listen to his lover's breath.

Chapter 12

The next day, Hunter felt the heat in his muscles as he moved across the dojo and worked through his kata. He knew this dojo well. It was his second refuge and one he'd come back to many, many times after moving to the city.

When he first started practicing, the sensei had seemed rather surprised by his interest in the martial arts. He'd never worked with a visually impaired person before and had doubts about his ability to train Hunter correctly. But four and a half years later, through many frustrating starts and stops, Hunter had attained his black belt. He enjoyed the freedom and sense of security it gave him. As an added benefit, it had given his mother some peace knowing he wasn't going to be so easily victimized in the big city.

But there was a simple reason he'd showed up at the dojo the first time. Someone claimed he wouldn't be able to get any further than the basic forms because of his blindness.

He'd been eating at a small but famous southern style restaurant on Ponce when he overheard an odd conversation between two men who were talking about martial arts. One of the men didn't agree that just anyone could learn the skills. Spying Hunter across the room, he used him as an example of a man who wouldn't be able to master anything but the most basic of forms.

Hunter initially sat in silent agreement with his assessment and thought nothing of it until later that night as he lay in bed. But then he asked himself why he'd so readily acquiesced to such an absurdly bigoted statement. While it seemed true that there was a substantial difference between learning the forms through rote and mastering them, the argument didn't preclude that he couldn't do it simply because he was blind.

Coming to the dojo was one of the best decisions he'd ever made, and was only validated when he overheard someone remark about that hard ass blind homo while he was sparring. He recalled the moment with a grin as he worked through his kata, then set himself adrift in the fluidity of movement, the sweat pouring off of him as he moved around the floor.

Normally, he had this time to himself since he took private lessons. But today, he heard a slight shift in the sound of the fan whirling on the opposite side of the room. He used the noise to orient himself and his opponents when they sparred. The way it shifted let him know he was no longer alone. Since the Sensei was in his office, it could only be a guest. He kept to his workout.

The fan pushed a waft of fresh outside air in his direction. Within that breath of air, he detected Dillon's curious aroma. He'd considered asking Dillon where it came from, but he liked the mystery of it and how the illusion of an exotic locale expressed itself every time Dillon was near. But now his balm stood out in the stale air of the dojo like a beacon, distracting him. But Hunter kept silent, wondering why he'd come. When Dillon took one of the spectator seats, he continued with his kata and lost himself in its flow once again.

Fifteen minutes later, his Sensei stepped on the mat and they sparred for a hard thirty minutes. When they were done, they bowed and Dillon thanked him before he turned in Dillon's direction.

"What are you doing here?"

"Came to watch my ninja," Dillon answered casually. "I hope you don't mind."

His ninja. Hunter liked that, a lot. "Not at all," he said as he came over.

"I was wondering if you'd like to come to my place. If you're not busy," he added quickly. "I thought I could make dinner."

"And after?" Hunter asked.

He heard Dillon get up and listened to his shoes squelch against the floor. He'd have to talk to him about that small breach of dojo etiquette later.

"We might think of something," Dillon answered quietly, a small kernel of desire buried under his voice.

"Let me get my stuff."

***

"You know, this is the first time I've done this," Hunter told him as they came into Dillon's condo. The condo was actually a luxury apartment in one of the swankiest parts of the city and way up on the twenty-sixth floor of a high rise. The whole complex literally smelled of money as soon as Hunter walked in the building. Dillon's apartment was no different.

"The first time you've done what?" Dillon asked.

"Gone to someone else's place like this. It's a little scary," Hunter admitted.

Dillon looked at him for a moment. "I promise I won't hurt you."

Hunter paused and turned to the sound of his voice. He reached out and cupped Dillon's cheek before he gently put a kiss on his lips. He didn't know what to say to that. It touched him too deep and too quickly. It was so honest and raw.

"I've moved a few things around for you," Dillon managed, breaking off the sudden yearning between them.

"So I don't break anything?" Hunter asked. His tone was suddenly snide.

A silence fell between them before Dillon spoke again. His voice was tight and controlled. "We need to get something straight. I don't do the pity party for anyone. I don't know if that's because of my job, or my past or what. I don't do it. For you, I won't do it, precisely because I know how much it bothers you, and I can respect that. But I wouldn't do it because I also happen to like you, a lot. So can we not have this type of conversation again? I know you can take care of yourself. Hell, I saw you whip that dude's ass on the street. I don't think my little ninja needs to be coddled like a two-year-old."

"But you moved things out of the way," Hunter insisted, the accusation lingering.

Dillon blew out a breath. "I inherited this apartment. I moved

Shawn's ashes because they were on a pedestal in front of the window and I thought it would be disrespectful if I had to clean them up with the vacuum. Not to mention your embarrassment."

Hunter's mouth snapped shut with a click of his teeth. It opened and closed again before he could form a sentence. "I'm sorry. Did I tell you I can be an over-sensitive, yet insensitive ass sometimes?"

"You may have mentioned that, yes."

"Margie can attest to it." He pulled Dillon to him and kissed his lips, his tongue slipping in before he pulled away. He reached down to take Dillon's hand. "Want to walk me around the room so I can navigate?"

Dillon shook his head. "You don't need me to do that. You'll probably have this whole apartment mapped out in ten minutes."

Hunter pressed up against him with a coquettish nuzzle into his sweet-smelling neck. "True, but I figured the last room would be the bedroom and we could, uh…explore it together. If you're with me, I don't have to fake a fall or knock all your shit off the dresser to get you in there."

Dillon started laughing. "You would do that too, wouldn't you?"

"Damned straight," Hunter murmured as he nibbled on his neck.

"How about I just follow behind?" Dillon asked. He stepped behind Hunter and nuzzled the back of Hunter's ear. "That stick of yours makes me nervous now that I've seen it in action."

Hunter leaned back against him and grinned. "You're lucky I don't use it on that cute butt," he whispered, teasing him with a small grope.

"Hmm, that could be interesting," he purred as he gently bit Hunter's earlobe.

They went around the perimeter of the big main room first. Dillon showed him where the light switches were and oriented him to the general layout of the room before Hunter did a grid sweep of the center of the apartment. It was an open floor plan and Hunter noticed right away that Dillon wasn't on his heels like he said he'd be. He stood back and let Hunter make his own mental map. "You've done this before," he said to Dillon.

"My cousin," Dillon reminded him. "He wouldn't let his mobility specialist from the school show him around. It always had to be me."

Hunter nodded in understanding. The condo was substantially larger than his apartment. It was almost a small townhome with two levels, a loft, and a huge kitchen. There were two bedrooms, two baths, and it had enough closet space that Hunter thought his apartment could probably fit into them if broken into small chunks.

"This place is massive," Hunter said after he had a map of it in his head. "I don't know why you'd want to move. You told me you were apartment hunting."

Dillon shrugged. "I don't really need all this space. My old apartment would've fit into the bathroom. I just had a little efficiency. I still don't know what to do with it."

"Would you mind if I grabbed a shower before we explore the bedroom in depth?" Hunter asked.

"I thought you liked a little aroma kink," Dillon teased him.

"I do." Hunter lifted his shirt near his arm and sniffed at it. "But this is straight funk, and that's so not going to work."

"Sure, I'll get dinner started while you shower."

"Did you bring up my bag? I think I left it in the car."

"Got it," Dillon took it from the corner and put it in his hand.

***

Dillon watched as Hunter went to the bathroom. He shook his head. Every second he spent with this guy made the small ache in his chest grow exponentially. And yet, they both seemed to be walking around on eggshells. "What the fuck?" he asked himself quietly. What was the sense in stepping to the edge of desire before suddenly pulling back? It made no sense. That was the problem. He was in way too deep and afraid to go any further, despite the decisions he'd already made.

He looked toward the bathroom, wondering if dinner had been such a good idea. Hell, maybe a blind man and an ex-prostitute getting together wasn't good idea at all. It was pretty obvious they both still had some serious hang-ups to overcome.

He went to the stereo and put on some music, making sure that the speakers for both the bathroom and the master bedroom were on. He smiled to think of Hunter laughing in the toilet, the sudden romance falling down on him. It wasn't too far removed from how Dillon felt at that moment. His feelings for Hunter kept falling down on him like an inescapable rain. He kept getting drenched, not sure if he wanted to dance in it or pop open an umbrella and run for cover.

"You're such an idiot," he told himself quietly.

"I like that!" Hunter yelled about the music.

He smiled. He was overthinking things again. He needed to just stop and let things unfold.

He went to the kitchen and started pulling dinner together. Earlier in the day, he'd gone shopping and had already prepped most of their meal. The farmer's market had been bursting with so many exotic little spices that he'd bought enough for ten meals. But in the end, he settled on a fresh fish that only needed minimal seasoning.

The whole excursion ended up as a ridiculous excuse to spend money. But what the hell, if Hunter let him, he planned on doing a lot more entertaining. That meant he needed to have something in his cupboards besides Cheerios and non-fat milk.

Maybe he'd take a cooking class or two. He certainly had the time now. And if anything, his culinary attempts would be a great excuse to spend more time with Hunter. He'd need a guinea pig after all. He smirked at the thought of it. A cooking class…

He listened to the water start and overheard Hunter exclaiming about the obscene size of the bathroom when an arousing thought came into his mind – something steamy and wet and hot. His smirk grew to a broad grin as he started taking his shirt off and made his way to the bathroom. Another hour before dinner got started wouldn't hurt anything, not at all.

He stripped his clothes off outside the bathroom and looked in. Hunter hadn't closed the door and because of the fans, most of the steam from the dual shower heads was being drawn out into the world instead of falling into the apartment.

Dillon gazed at Hunter from the door, the clear glass of the enclosed shower making him look like a Greek god wrapped in cellophane. Jesus, he's beautiful, Dillon thought as he watched him. The steam surrounded Hunter like a shroud, a grey-white blanket caressing his skin as he lathered and soaped himself. The lines on his body were so masculine and beautiful that Dillon could not understand for the life of him why Hunter was still single.

But was he single? Dillon didn't really know, and if he was honest with himself, he didn't want to know. But he didn't think Hunter was the kind of person who would lead him on if he were attached. He couldn't explain it, but Hunter seemed too real to be playing the field – too faithful to be hurting people just to feed his ego.

He swallowed, his eyes lingering as Hunter washed his hair and tilted his head back. His semi-erect cock was swaying in the steam, mesmerizing Dillon as if it were a cobra about to strike. And here he was gawking, invading Hunter's privacy like some adolescent voyeur. He cleared his throat loud enough to make sure Hunter knew he was there.

Hunter smiled. "I was hoping you'd show up."

"Can I join you?" Dillon asked, watching the two opposite

heads of the shower rain down on Hunter's magnificent body.

"Of course."

"I was watching you," Dillon admitted as he stepped into the shower.

"That's why I left the door open, silly. You think because I'm blind I don't know how to bait a sightling?" Hunter asked as he pulled Dillon to him and started sucking on his ear.

Dillon laughed, tilted his head back, and purred as the steam built up around them. "I think you are the smartest goddamn man I ever met," Dillon admitted. He was spellbound. He just had to find the nuts to admit it openly.

Hunter's cock was sandwiched between them, hot and swollen, matching his own as Hunter continued to suck and chew and nibble on his neck. He loved that Hunter was such an oral person.

Music floated down from the speakers as Hunter stood fully and took Dillon's face in his hands. He pressed their lips together, the raw heat of his breath stealing away any stops Dillon might have fleetingly considered.

Dillon pressed his hands to Hunter's chest as they kissed, feeling his heartbeat, the raw power of him. Hunter took his breath, stole it away with his heart, and captured it within his jaws. He could taste the fire of Hunter's lust as if it were a palatable thing – something he could whip up in the kitchen, or the bedroom, or right here in the bath.

His breath rumbled in his chest as Hunter released his lips

and started working down his torso. He bit his bottom lip and drew in a hard breath when Hunter took his cock in his mouth. Hunter moved on it slow, licking at the head, making Dillon curl his hands into his hair and beg for more. Dillon's whole body tingled with the sensations Hunter's tongue brought from within him.

That was the thing with Hunter. It wasn't just sex. It was a whole sensory experience – every single touch, every kiss, every nibble. Hunter was like a lightning bolt and Dillon's body throbbed every time Hunter caressed him. He ached for his touch like he ached for life itself. Dillon's body had never reacted like that before.

He looked down when Hunter let go of his cock and watched as he reached out, found the soap, and gently began to wash it. He groaned at the sensual cleaning, the soft motions Hunter made with his hands, and the flexing grip Hunter held him with.

Hunter stood and continued to stroke him. He took his free hand and pulled Dillon's mouth closer, an open ache registering as he met Dillon's lips. When he released Dillon, he soaped up his own backside, turned to face the wall of the shower and spread himself against it, waiting to be filled and loved and taken.

Dillon's balls ached at the sight of him. He moved in slowly, slipping himself between Hunter's thighs as he let his desire rise. He wanted to cherish this sight. If he and Hunter never developed a relationship, he'd never forget this beautiful man aching to be loved against his shower wall. Maybe this was how Hunter felt when he'd fucked Dillon against the wall of his apartment the last time they were together. And maybe this was a test to see what Dillon had learned on that extraordinary night.

He kissed Hunter's neck as he slid fully into him, the soap such an easy lube, the need making the pain a thing that didn't exist. He touched Hunter's chest and held himself still, his hands caressing Hunter's abdomen before he began any pelvic motion.

And still the music floated down.

Dillon soaped up his right hand and reached around to grasp the hot flesh between Hunter's legs. He caressed him as he wrapped his fingers around the thick base of Hunter's cock. While he drew his hand up and down the length of Hunter's shaft, he sank his cock deeper into Hunter's ass, pushing Hunter to the wall, trapping Hunter's sex inside his soap-slicked hand.

He fucked Hunter slow, pressing into him so that Hunter's cock slid back and forth in his hand as they moved together. Their heat pushed the steam from around them and created more – a small ring around their longing.

He licked at Hunter's neck and kissed it as they moved together. He stroked Hunter's ear with his tongue and pressed all his hopes and dreams forward through every pore of his body, hoping Hunter would understand without him having to speak the words.

They came with a silent, powerful shudder. The music wafting down was all the noise they needed. Their bodies tensed with the desperate urgency they both felt inside. Hunter leaned back into him without a word, the gentle might of their mutual orgasm so satisfying that all he could do was sag in Dillon's arms.

***

Hunter turned and kissed Dillon deeply before he rinsed off. He'd never wished for his sight before, but he would've given anything at that moment to be able to turn and witness the beauty of the man who had just made love to him. He'd literally felt the change in Dillon's grip as he made love.

The first time they were together, Dillon's hold was uncertain – a tentative embrace that held no absolutes, no dreams. But just now it was different. It was a grip that sat right on the edge of possession. A possession Hunter would've gladly given if asked.

Chapter 13

Hunter planned to have lunch with Margie the following Friday so he could introduce Dillon. But he hadn't planned on Lydia calling at the last minute with an announcement that she was coming to the city and wanted to take Hunter out for dinner.

It was a complete first for Lydia. Typically, she just showed up unannounced and expected Hunter to drop everything. Since Hunter had his own business and "had no love life," this was usually not a problem. Usually.

"I wanted to confirm lunch for Friday," Hunter said when he phoned Margie later.

"Yep, we're still on. Unless something's come up?" she asked, her tone insinuating.

"Lydia called," Hunter told her. "She's coming in on Friday and wants to have dinner."

"So? What's wrong with that?"

"This can't be good."

"Maybe she just wants to tell you about the new man in her life," Margie suggested.

Hunter groaned. "I don't want to meet Lydia's boyfriend or even know about him." Lydia had been his single, controlling mother for thirty years. He simply couldn't see her in any other way. "And what if this guy is a douchebag? I'd be tempted to stomp him right there in the middle of the restaurant."

"From what you've said, I don't think your mom would allow that type of guy in her life."

"I can't do it alone. Why don't you come with me?" he begged.

"No way, no how. Your mother is a grown, independent woman. Get used to it. I'll see you and your lover boy at lunch," she'd added before she hung up.

His lover-boy, yes. Now there was an idea. He could introduce Dillon at the same time. Maybe two new boyfriends together would balance each other out. And Dillon could keep him entertained and be on hand if the guy was an asshole.

He called Dillon next.

"I don't know, Hunter," Dillon replied when Hunter explained his reason for calling.

A lump came up in his throat. He was pushing. Here he was asking Dillon to meet his mother like they had something serious together. Meeting Margie was one thing, but meeting the rents, that had entirely different connotations. "I'm sorry. I didn't mean to imply…"

"It's not that," Dillon interrupted. He sighed at length. "This isn't going to be a big blowout between you two or anything, is it?" he asked. "I'm really not any good at being a referee."

Hunter was silent for a moment, wondering where that comment had come from. At first, he thought it might have something to do with his bitching about Lydia being somewhat overprotective, but he quickly came to realize that it wasn't that at all. Dillon's tone seemed... It was hard to place. It was almost as if he was more concerned about the possibility of Hunter asking to meet his family.

And that made sense. Dillon never spoke about his personal life. Not that Hunter expected it. But all the curt silences and abruptly ended sentences alluded to whatever had prompted Dillon to the streets, and Hunter would've bet money that it had to do with his family. But obviously, he couldn't come right out and ask. Nor could he say that he didn't want to meet Dillon's family because that was another conversation which had too much innuendo.

"No blowouts. I just really need your help on this one," he told Dillon finally. He laughed, trying to lighten the conversation. "And my mother would never allow an argument in public. Her Southern ancestors would haunt me for the rest of my life if that happened."

Dillon was silent for a moment. "Okay, I'll go."

"Thanks," Hunter answered with relief.

"I'll pick you up at eleven for lunch then we can mess around for a few hours before dinner with your mom," Dillon said. "How's that?"

"That sounds interesting."

Dillon laughed. "Don't even. If you think I'm going to meet your mom all sweaty and smelling like jizz, you're crazy. You're going to have to promise to behave yourself during intermission."

"Intermission?"

"You've got me on stage twice today, Hunter. Lunch with

Margie and dinner with your mom."

"Ah, sorry."

"Don't be," Dillon said gently. "Has to happen eventually, right? Maybe it's better that we can get it all done in one day."

The only way it would have to happen was if Dillon was considering something a little more serious. Hunter beamed at the thought. "I'll make it up to you," he promised quietly.

"You already have. See you in a few hours," Dillon answered before he hung up.

Hunter put the phone down. What had he done to deserve something like this, someone like him? Hunter knew people saw him as a mean, self-centered prick, and most days that was true. So what grace had he been given to deserve someone who could melt your soul away like Dillon did?

He clucked his tongue, unable to figure it out.

***

Hunter's stomach was rumbling when they got to the Rat Hole, but it wasn't from hunger. He was nervous. As much as he disliked what Margie had said about Dillon, Hunter needed her approval. He couldn't say exactly why, but he also knew her opinion would be an important factor in making a decision about how serious he was going to get. He might have told himself otherwise, but when it came right down to it, he didn't want to have to choose between them. He needed Margie and he was beginning to need Dillon more and more.

That wasn't entirely true either. He needed to stop fooling

himself about the people in his life. Margie's impression was important because Margie was more than just a friend. She was like the sister Hunter never had, the older sibling he could bounce ideas and problems off of and get an honest response without all his mother's judgment and generational garbage mixed in.

He wanted Margie to like Dillon and accept him as much as she had accepted Hunter's blindness. So what if he was a prostitute? He was still someone Hunter cared about, right?

He was so tense that he stopped just outside the door. Dillon bumped into him from behind and steadied himself by grabbing Hunter's shoulders.

"What's wrong?" Dillon asked.

Hunter licked his lips. "I'm nervous all of a sudden," he admitted without confessing that this meeting was really about common sense and logic over emotion. He was desperately lonely; even though he was loath to admit it. But by coming here, he was using Margie as a gauge against putting his vulnerability out there. If she said Dillon wasn't the right guy for him, what would he do? Was he really going to concede to her assessment and tell Dillon to take a hike?

It was pretty lame when he considered it, particularly with how much he pranced around about his independence like it could isolate him from his loneliness somehow. But maybe that was the root of it. Maybe he'd been using the stink of independence to cover up his loneliness. Maybe that was why he'd turned into an obnoxious jackass. He shook the thought from his head. All he wanted was his friend and his lover to get along like a nice, big, happy family. That wasn't too much to ask, was it?

"It's okay," Dillon reassured him. "What's the worst she could do with my little ninja here to protect me?"

Hunter smiled. "Could we just keep that one between us? I'd never hear the end of it."

Dillon laughed and opened the door. The warmth of the place spilled out into the cooling November air.

"Damn, what's a fine ass white boy like you doing in here?" Connie said when she looked up and saw Dillon coming through the door. Every head in the place swiveled in their direction as he pointed at Hunter.

"You're with Batman?" she asked Dillon, her surprise evident.

He nodded.

"Damn, I'm impressed," she barked at Hunter and started laughing. "I didn't think you had it in you. Corner table," she instructed. She pointed at it for Dillon's sake.

Hunter cringed inside. Maybe he'd been worrying about the wrong person. "Thanks, Connie," he mumbled and asked Dillon to direct him to their table.

They usually had the same table every time he came in, but sometimes when it was busy, as it sounded to him now, he was put wherever there was space. Connie was always his waitress.

"Batman?" Dillon whispered as they sat down.

"Long story."

"This one, I've got to hear." Dillon chuckled as he looked across the table and met a set of stern, evaluating eyes. He remembered the look from his youth. It was the same one he'd worn when he thought someone might be a threat to Travis. It was a look which said trust would be earned the hard way before any sanction was given.

He reached across the table, his hand out. "You must be Margie. Hunter's said so much about you."

Her eyes narrowed in suspicion. She glanced at his hand before she reached out and shook it. "I'm sure he has."

"Come on, Margie. I said I was sorry," Hunter objected.

She had her eyes on Dillon. "Yeah, you did."

Connie came to the table and gave Dillon another appreciative glance before she took their orders. She threw a few more banters back and forth with Hunter and disappeared with a laugh. Hunter got the impression that this was going to be a very long lunch.

Dillon took Connie's banter in stride and chuckled when she left. But Connie's and Margie's initial reactions already had Hunter asking himself what he was doing.

Was he trying to make Dillon prove his worth? For what? For him? For Margie? As if Dillon didn't have any self-worth and Hunter had to throw him up on a stage for the approval of his friends. What kind of shithead did that make him? If someone had done that to him, he'd have been screaming at them already.

Dillon suddenly ran his fingers across the top of Hunter's

knuckles, as if he'd heard every insecure thought and was silently reassuring him of their inaccuracy. Hunter put his other hand over Dillon's and held him for a moment. He'd needed that small contact.

***

"Hunter says you're an escort." Margie started the conversation.

Dillon glanced at Hunter. He looked like she'd kicked him in the balls, as if he wanted to crawl under the table or reach over and choke her.

Honestly, Dillon wasn't sure which scene would give him more satisfaction. He hadn't been ambushed like that in years.

From beside him, he felt Hunter's anger flare and had no doubt Margie also saw the harsh rebuke sitting on the edge of his lips. He was keeping cool only because he was waiting for Dillon's reaction.

But Dillon was actually happy that Hunter told her. It got all of the potential lies and worries out of the way right up front. "That's true," he answered her.

"Are you still?" she asked.

"Yes," he answered quietly. He didn't mean to lie. The word just fell out of his mouth. He still hadn't figured out how he'd talk to Hunter about the fact that he'd left the profession and he certainly didn't want to start the conversation here.

She narrowed her eyes at him again, studying him as she spoke. "Hunter likes you, a lot."

Dillon smiled and turned to him, brushing his index finger lightly across Hunter's cheek. "Is that true?" he asked quietly. Maybe there was hope for them yet.

"Not the way I had envisioned saying it, but yeah, that's true," Hunter answered, the little piqué in his voice directed at Margie.

Margie ignored him, put her elbow on the table, and pointed directly at Dillon. "If you hurt him I'm going to cut your fucking heart out."

"Margie!" Hunter erupted, a tight anger in his voice.

"She's okay," Dillon answered lightly. He knew where this was coming from. She'd expected him to be a fraud and he wasn't living up to her expectations. He liked that it was happening so quickly, but Hunter was irate that she was so rude about it.

He looked directly at Margie, not doubting her seriousness for a moment. He'd felt exactly the same about Travis and suddenly he wondered why. Was it because he'd thought Travis was inferior, like he needed protection? The thought gave him pause. Odd that she'd made him take note of his subliminal discrimination. No wonder Hunter seemed angry about people's perceptions so often.

"I don't have any plans on hurting him on purpose," Dillon told her. "But I can't promise it won't happen by accident."

She nodded after a moment. "Fair enough. I'm sure he'll do the same to you once or twice."

Connie came over and interrupted the conversation, her elbows in everyone's face as she plopped down the daily specials they'd ordered. She gave Dillon another once over and glanced at Hunter and Margie with a shake of her head. "What's a beautiful hunk of man like you doing hanging out with Batman and Robin here?" she asked Dillon.

Dillon looked up at her. "If I wasn't already taken," he said with a small smile, "I might be looking for a fine woman like you."

"Sheeeut," she said with a little giggle that almost made Hunter fall off his chair in shock. "You wouldn't have to look far. Or long. Likes me some fine white boys."

"He's taken," Hunter piped up, his finger in the air for emphasis.

A small but knowing sneer turned her mouth sideways. "All the good ones are. Y'all enjoy," she said before she walked off.

"Did she just tell us to enjoy our food?" Margie asked, aghast.

Hunter laughed. He had to. It was all so absurd, the whole ridiculous situation. "I think you just tamed the beast," he told Dillon.

"Nah, she's a pushover," Dillon answered. "Unlike Margie here, who probably would cut my nuts off," he said as he glanced across the table again.

"What are your thoughts about love?" Margie asked out of nowhere. She picked up the ketchup and poured some on her fries, gallantly trying to make the question seem innocent.

"Margie," Hunter warned. "You're putting a little much into this aren't you? We're just having lunch. It's not an engagement party."

"Am I?" she asked Hunter in return. "But that's not why I asked. I thought with his… business, he might have a different perspective." She looked at Dillon, searching his eyes out.

Dillon saw her intent immediately. She was trying to show Hunter how feckless he was about love because he was an escort. He felt Hunter tense, but whether that was in further anger at her for grilling him, or because he was unsure about Dillon's answer seemed open to debate.

He honestly didn't know how he felt about it. He'd never thought about it before, and certainly never dared to hope he'd experience it. He took the salt shaker, sprinkled a little on the table top, and then drew a circle in it. "I'll tell you what a friend told me," he said, directing her attention to the circle and explaining what he'd done to Hunter.

"He said we all have this different idea of what love is, and that's what makes our circle. The more ideas and misconceptions you throw in, the larger the diameter and the harder it is to connect with someone. We," he said, squeezing Hunter's hand and signaling Margie and everyone around them, "all sit around the edge looking at everyone else around the circle. Sometimes we just settle for the person next to us because it's easy or convenient. Then we skip our way around its circumference, never really knowing what love is all about."

He took a sip of his Coke and kept his eyes on Margie. "But other times, you see the person across from you, staring back at you.

You fight like hell trying to get across while he does the same. If you're lucky, there's a rope you can toss over and help draw each other in. You never look away, never worry about those people still wandering around the circumference. It's just you and him, pulling each other in deeper and deeper."

He took his finger off the table and licked the salt off.

***

Margie looked from the circle to Dillon and back again. She'd been enraptured with his small parable. It was so…beautiful. She wanted to ask him where he thought he and Hunter stood in that circular environment, but it was so frigging obvious that she was honestly a little jealous. And yet, looking at the two of them together, she saw that neither of them could see it for themselves. They were both still sitting on the edge of the circle holding the rope but afraid to tug on it. What the hell were they waiting for?

Whatever it was, she decided right then and there that she wasn't getting into the middle of it. They'd have to figure it out on their own.

"Well?" Hunter asked.

"Okay, fuck. He seems like a keeper," she told Hunter. "But my warning still stands," she said with a warning finger waving at Dillon.

Hunter smiled while Dillon did a small victory jig in his seat. "One down, one to go," he told Hunter.

Margie looked at him in question.

"Meeting Hunter's mom tonight," Dillon explained.

"Oh," Margie said. She looked over at Hunter who suddenly seemed intensely focused on his plate. "Oh."

***

Dillon laughed when they got back to Hunter's apartment. "Jesus, she was a little intense. I hope your mom isn't that bad."

"I've never seen that side of Margie," Hunter admitted. "But you won her over." He slid next to Dillon and pulled him into an embrace. "That story about the circle…" Hunter started without finishing. He put his head on Dillon's shoulder, listening to his heartbeat. He drank in his warm strength as Dillon's arms encircled him.

"What about it?"

"Is that really what you believe?" Hunter asked cautiously.

"Honestly?"

Hunter pulled his head from Dillon's shoulder and reached out for his cheek, cupping it as he sought more than the assured rhythm of his voice. "Yes," he answered quietly, a desperate plea in his voice.

"I didn't," Dillon replied. "But that's changed. I didn't even remember the story until she asked that question, and then what Shu-shu said just popped into my head and made sense." He looked at Hunter. "You made it make sense."

This was the second time Dillon had mentioned Shu-shu. The man seemed to have had a significant effect on Dillon's life. Yet, Dillon still kept that part of himself hidden. Maybe that would change with time. He sought Dillon's lips, running his thumb across them before he leaned forward. "You're beautiful," he murmured before he pressed in with something slow and gentle.

Dillon sighed when Hunter pulled away. "You could kill me with those lips."

Hunter smiled and leaned forward again. "Slowly, very slowly."

Dillon melted into him, sucking on his offered tongue, brushing his lips over Hunter's chin, up his jaw, back down to the luscious lips again. He sighed as Hunter kissed him back. He loved the velvety soft texture against his skin.

"Didn't you say your mom was coming over to pick us up for dinner?" he reminded Hunter.

"I'll make her wait outside until we're done."

Dillon pushed him back and chuckled. "What a great first impression that would make."

Hunter adjusted the erection in his pants. "Yes, well, she can be very inconvenient at times."

"How did I get roped into this again?" Dillon asked.

"It was just supposed to be Margie, but my mother only comes up about once every three months, so I couldn't really say no. You can go home, you don't have to stay. I just thought…" he shrugged. He wasn't convincing either of them and he knew it.

Dillon pulled him into his arms again. "I'm not going anywhere. And now that you have me all worked up I'd just have to go home and jerk off anyway."

Hunter snaked his hand down immediately, cupping Dillon's

stiffness in his palm. "Maybe after we come back from dinner?"

"Didn't you tell me your mom's staying here for the night?"

"Yes, she usually does. But we can go somewhere. Your place or a motel, it doesn't matter to me."

Dillon laughed at his incorrigibility. "No, down, boy," he said, pushing Hunter back again. "You'd never hear the end of it for leaving her here, and I'd be in the dog house for sure."

Hunter put on a pouty face, crossed his arms and slouched like a reprimanded child. "Can we sit on the couch and cuddle then? A little necking never hurt anyone."

"That will only get us in trouble. How about I make us some tea?" Dillon asked as he stepped around him and headed for the kitchen. "You have tea?"

"Yeah, it's in the cupboard there somewhere. I don't drink the stuff, but my mother insists I have it when she comes. Coffee for me," Hunter called to him.

He went to the couch and sat down, listening to Dillon hum to himself in the kitchen. He liked the fact that Dillon seemed so comfortable, but wondered if he'd be upset when he learned that Hunter hadn't bothered to tell Lydia he'd be joining them.

Hunter hoped not. By inviting Dillon, Hunter hoped to make Lydia see beyond her depreciating view of normal and realize that just because her son was blind; it didn't mean that he lived a life of boyfriend-less solitude. And if he had to meet her new boyfriend, well then, she was going to meet Dillon.

Dillon came back into the room. "Coffee's on."

"Thanks," Hunter said as he patted the couch.

Dillon sat down next to him and took his hand. Hunter felt it and unexpectedly began mulling over the question of how many of Dillon's previous clients had spent 'off time' with him. Did they tell him they wanted him permanently? Did they say they'd take care of him and take him away from hustling? How many had done that? Dozens, hundreds perhaps? And how many honestly tempted him with that query? How many sheets had Dillon been between where he wondered if the person next to him was the one who'd take him away? Had he ever? Would he ever?

He couldn't hustle his ass forever, but was he ready to leave it now? Would he leave it for a thirty-year-old blind man who had nothing to offer but his heart? Would he if their positions were reversed?

Chapter 14

The phone rang while Dillon was pouring coffee in the kitchen. Already tense, Hunter reached over and grabbed it. He knew this couldn't be good.

"Can we meet at the restaurant instead?" Lydia asked. "You can get there on your own, can't you?"

"Yes, mother. Somehow I've managed to navigate the entire city all by myself when you're not here."

"Fine," Lydia replied and clicked off.

Hunter put the phone down and started chewing on the corner of his lip. He should've told her he was bringing Dillon. But, once again, Lydia had pushed his buttons before they could get into the meat of the conversation.

"She wants to meet at the restaurant," Hunter muttered out loud, lost in his sudden uneasiness about the topic of this dinner.

"Okay," Dillon said as he came from the kitchen with Hunter's coffee in hand. "I know right where the restaurant is. No problem." He looked at Hunter a little closer and noticed the expression on his face. "That is okay, isn't it?"

"Um, yes. My mom's just acting a little weird," Hunter answered vaguely.

Dillon reached for his hand and steered it to the coffee mug. "It's hot, be careful."

Hunter took it and nodded without comment. He took a sip and smiled. "You make good coffee." He said before his expression went bleak again.

"What's wrong?" Dillon asked.

He sat a small distance away and Hunter reached out and rubbed his free hand along Dillon's thigh. "I'm worried about what she's going to say. I thought..." He turned to Dillon's light breathing. "I thought she might be inviting me to meet a new man in her life, but now I'm not so sure. She's acting so...off."

Dillon tilted his head and studied him for a moment. "So this might be something important. Does she know I'm coming?"

Hunter shook his head. "Sorry."

Dillon put his tea down on the end table and opened his mouth to say something before he closed it again. "That's not cool," he managed, a slight edge in his voice.

"I know," Hunter replied. "You don't have to go. It was selfish and rude of me to do that to you." He sighed. "I'm sorry."

Dillon watched him for a moment longer. He looked scared. "What do you think she's going to say?" he asked quietly.

The hollow silence of Hunter's stillness filled the space between them.

"My mom and I have never been the best of friends," Hunter admitted. "And she was acting really weird when I went home last time. I thought it was a man in her life, but now I'm not so sure."

What if she was dying and trying to figure out a way to tell him? Maybe she hadn't been ready to tell him when he went home.

Lydia had never been the overly emotional type, and a restaurant where she'd absolutely forbid a scene would be the place she'd make the announcement. And knowing her, she'd pop it out like they were talking about the taxes on the house. *Hunter, my time is up. I've left the papers with Gerald. The funeral's paid for and I need you to sign right here.*

"I'll go," Dillon offered when his silence lengthened.

Hunter shook his head. "You can just drop me off, or I can catch a cab. You don't have to."

"I'll go," Dillon insisted. He knew what it was like to lose a parental anchor in life. And while Hunter's experience wouldn't be anywhere near as traumatic as his own had been; it didn't mean it would affect him any less.

***

When they arrived a few hours later, the young hostess greeted them but didn't know what to make of Hunter.

The girl smelled of bubble gum and tits and Hunter disliked her immediately. She was probably some snobby, preppy college girl who'd never seen a blind man in her life and wanted to treat him like a child. It was one of the biggest reasons Hunter never visited chain restaurants. It was the same food, same staff, and same obnoxious yet unintentional bigotries. He hated it. But Lydia insisted on these innocuous dumps because the food was familiar and safe. She knew about Hunter's gastronomic explorations in the city and wanted no part of them.

He was about to say something and shred the hostess to

pieces, but Dillon stepped around him and took command. He clamped his mouth shut and followed Ms. Bubble Gum Tits to the table like a meek little puppy. He didn't want to make a scene. He'd already put Dillon on the spot with this dinner, there was no sense in making it worse.

"She's here alone," Dillon muttered as they made their way to the table.

His heart sank. "Mom," he said as he sat down.

"I didn't realize you were bringing company," Lydia said as she looked Dillon up and down.

"This is Dillon. Dillon, my mom."

***

Dillon nodded and reached across the table to shake her hand. "Ma'am. It's a pleasure to meet you."

Lydia was of the same Southern pedigree as his mother – her poise, the dress, and the lady-like movements. But Dillon didn't see the anger in her eyes or disgust. He saw a gentle preoccupation with her son and a curious appraisal of the man he'd brought with him. He relaxed immediately. This dinner didn't have anything to do with her death.

"Well, at least he has manners," Lydia said with a slight tilt of her head.

Hunter was fidgeting beside him, still thinking his mother was gravely ill. Dillon reached under the table and let his hand rest on Hunter's leg. Hunter latched onto it immediately.

Dillon cleared his throat. "Mrs. Stephens, I don't want to

seem too forward, but Hunter seems to think you're ill. That's why I'm here."

Her face opened up and she nodded in understanding. "Well, I'm glad he has someone to come to for emotional support…"

"So, you are sick," Hunter groaned.

"No, I'm not. I told you that at the house."

Hunter sat limp with relief. "Then why are we here?"

The waitress interrupted them with menus and ordering and drinks. Dillon ordered a bottle of wine with Lydia's approval and Hunter let him pick out his meal, knowing that whatever it was it would be as bland and tasteless as the décor he couldn't see. He just wanted the woman gone so he could get an answer to his question.

After the waitress left, Lydia grabbed a bag from under the table. "Oh, this is for you."

Hunter froze. "What is it?"

"The usual," Lydia answered with a smirk. She glanced at Dillon.

Dillon reached over the table and took the bag from her, putting it between their chairs. "The usual?" Dillon asked.

"Underwear," Hunter mumbled, the mortification of it lessening down to humor as he heard Dillon trying to stifle a chuckle from beside him. "I must be the only thirty-year-old homo who can't buy his own drawers."

"It's what a mother does," Lydia said. "Isn't that right?" she asked Dillon.

Dillon nodded with a smile but felt a sudden stab of

unexpected pain from her comment. "Yes, ma'am."

"See," she told Hunter. "You're lucky. I could be buying you Barney undies for the big boys. You'd never know."

Dillon burst out laughing. Hunter turned three shades of red.

But once again, Hunter realized that under her words, this wasn't the same woman he'd grown up with. She was more relaxed and carefree. Her happiness was evident, and the relaxed humor was something new. He sighed internally. Maybe Margie was right. Maybe it was time he grew up and took it to heart that Lydia had a life too. It was time to stop being the selfish, blind gay boy she'd raised.

The wine arrived and Dillon directed the waitress over to Lydia first. Hunter smiled. If nothing else, Dillon certainly knew how to win over the ladies. When Lydia acknowledged that the wine was good, the waitress poured and left the bottle on the table. Hunter wanted a more adult beverage but figured if it made these two happy he wouldn't complain.

"So," Hunter said.

"So," Lydia replied. She seemed as nervous as Hunter.

"You met someone."

"Yes," she answered uncomfortably. Obviously, explaining a new man in her life to her gay son wasn't in the Southern Belle handbook.

Hunter heard her take a sip of wine and listened to the slight tinkle of her ring against the glass. He'd bought it when he was eleven after winning a hundred dollars in a contest at school. She'd worn it ever since.

"He's twenty-four," she said quietly. "And blind."

Hunter was sure he misheard her. "What?"

"He's twenty-four. He teaches at the blind school."

"What?" Hunter repeated. His hand immediately sought Dillon's leg under the table.

His mother was a cougar. What the fuck? Dillon put his hand on top of Hunter's and caressed it with his thumb, quietly letting him know that his response wasn't appropriate.

"I'd like you to meet him," Lydia informed him. "But I thought we should talk first and discuss any problems you might have with our relationship."

Relationship? "Like he's twenty-four kind of problems?" Hunter reached for his wine and gulped down what was left of it. What was next? Was she going to tell him the kid was going to be his new stepdad? Twenty-four? He clamped his mouth shut and squeezed Dillon's hand under the table, quietly appreciating his presence. He wiped his mouth with his napkin, trying to collect himself. "Does he make you happy?" he asked, his voice a tight string of syllables.

She seemed to sigh a little before she answered. Hunter wanted to barf. Some kid was porking his mother and she was sighing like Scarlett O'Hara.

"Yes, he does," Lydia told him.

"So the baking…all that was for him?" Hunter asked politely.

"Yes, the ladies think it's time I stepped out again," she told

Hunter. "And I have."

Oh, she had, all right. There was no doubt about that in Hunter's mind. She'd stepped right out and then into bed with someone six years younger than he was.

The ladies were a group of old southern hens who Lydia had known forever. They knew everyone and everyone's business. They quilted for the church bazaars, baked for the Scout fundraisers and protected the dignity of their Southern lineage. Hunter detested most of the genteel bigotry they stood for and overlooked. But he also knew his mother was a part of that generation. For most of his life, he'd swallowed his bile about how he felt about their hypocrisy. But there was no sense in bringing it up now.

"And what do they think of him?" Hunter asked.

She tittered and Hunter almost groaned out load. He pictured some southern hunky man-stud who all the ladies were gaga over. He knew if the hens were squawking about his attributes and telling Lydia to go for it... He shook his head at the unfinished thought. He didn't want to know the details.

"So how did you meet?" Dillon interjected, quietly trying to pry Hunter's fingers from the tight grip they had on his leg.

"The ladies suggested I find something to do since my son couldn't be bothered to visit or call. Henrietta, she's a dear friend," she told Dillon, "suggested I try volunteering at the blind school Hunter went to. They always need help and since I had the experience..." She shrugged. "You'll like him, Hunter," she said. "He has no problem with gays."

Hunter tilted his head back and drew a deep breath. He could've face palmed himself or slammed his head on the table at that moment, but went for the less dramatic move instead. "That's sweet of him," he said as he leveled his head in Lydia's direction. "Maybe we can both date him. I mean, he is six years younger than me."

"How dare you," Lydia seethed.

"Is he a gold-digger?" Hunter snarled.

"Maybe I should…" Dillon said as he started to rise from the table.

"Sit!" Lydia and Hunter barked at the same time, squaring off.

Hunter drew a deep breath. He'd promised Dillon this wasn't going to be an argument. "So when do I meet him?"

"I don't think you're ready," Lydia snapped.

"You don't think…" He pressed his lips into a thin line. He should never have made that promise to Dillon. The fucking kid was twenty-four. "What's his name?" he asked, feigning a more casual attitude.

"Travis," she answered. "Travis Masters. I thought we could have Thanksgiving together. But obviously…"

Hunter winced in pain as Dillon squeezed his hand to the point of agony. Both he and Lydia heard Dillon's quick intake of breath. Hunter could feel the sudden tension from the seat next to him. It was like a grenade went off. "What the hell?"

"Do you know him?" Lydia asked Dillon.

***

Dillon's phone rang suddenly and they froze. It rang twice more before he pulled it from his belt. "Sorry, I forgot to turn it off," he told Hunter. Normally, he had it set on vibrate when they were together, but he'd forgotten all about it.

"Yes?" he asked as he brought the phone to his ear. He shrugged across the table at Lydia, who had raised her glass and was drinking her wine. It was obvious that she wasn't pleased with the interruption or the rudeness of answering the phone at the table, but she was polite enough not to say anything.

Hunter, on the other hand, was a bag of emotions. It was written so hard on his face that Dillon didn't understand why Lydia didn't see it. But then, she didn't know about Dillon's past and wouldn't be thinking what Hunter was. Likely, she assumed Hunter was still exasperating over Travis' age. He wondered if Hunter even noticed that she'd said he was blind.

"Thank you. I'll be right there," he replied before he hung up.

He stood before Hunter could grab his hand or dig his fingers back into his leg. "Mrs. Stephens it has been a pleasure to meet you, but I have a slight emergency."

She looked at him curiously and nodded but said nothing.

He turned to Hunter. "I...I'm sorry. I have to go."

"Client?" Hunter croaked, his voice full of venom and pain.

"Yes. I...I'm sorry, really. I... Can you get home all right?" He bent to kiss Hunter's forehead but thought better of it and stood. Hunter looked somewhere between completely crestfallen and utterly enraged.

Hunter's jaw clenched. "Yes."

Dillon snatched his coat from the back of the chair, nodded to Lydia again, and all but flew from the restaurant.

"What business is he in?" Lydia asked.

"Sales," Hunter mumbled.

***

The rest of their dinner was a blur. Dillon had paid for the check before he disappeared and left an enormous tip so the waitress would make sure they were well taken care of.

Hunter couldn't remember a single word his mother said after Dillon left. When she finally dropped him off in front of his apartment building, he'd gone upstairs and fallen on the couch with his coat still on. It never registered that she was driving back home in the dark, another first for her.

"What a goddamn idiot you are," he told himself. He reached for the phone, planning to call Margie, and then put it down again. He didn't want to hear her crow about how right she'd been. She'd warned him. He wouldn't be able to listen to her without exploding.

But he had no one to blame but himself. He knew who Dillon was up front. There had never been any deception. But the more he tried to move around the pain of that knowledge, the more it gouged into his skin. He'd hoped... Well, there was the problem wasn't it? He was just another victim of hope – that cursed thing that always fell short in the face of reality.

"Fuck!" he screamed into his empty apartment. He ripped his

coat off and threw it across the room before stalking into the kitchen. Somewhere in here there was a bottle of vodka and he intended to find it and get fucking wasted. Fuck work, fuck Margie, and fuck Dillon.

    He dug around in the cupboards before he remembered that he'd stashed it underneath the counter by the sink so Lydia wouldn't find it. When he pulled it out, he considered ice and a glass for a small second, but stomped back to the couch with just the bottle. He twisted the top off and brought it to his mouth. It was time to forget.

Chapter 15

Dillon ran from the restaurant and out to his car. This could not be happening. The chances were astronomical. It simply wasn't possible that his cousin had found the one woman in the entire world who just happened to be the mother of the man he was falling in love with. Not fucking possible. He sat in the car watching Hunter and his mother through the window. He wouldn't allow himself tears.

The call he'd received had been from his old service telling him he had a message. But he'd panicked when he heard Travis' name and told Hunter and Lydia a lie. He wasn't ready to deal with his family yet. He didn't know if he'd ever be, and he still hadn't figured out how he was going to answer all the questions that would come up about how he'd survived.

He slammed his hands on the steering wheel, started the car and started driving. He turned toward home, but as soon as he got on the interstate his mind wandered and he just let the car go where it wanted to. He ended up on I-285 going around the city. It went round and round, just like his life – one big fucking circle jerk which just kept coming back to the same starting point: his family.

Ten years after they tossed him out like trash, it still ate into him. He was still ashamed of what they'd done and what he'd had to do to survive. And now Travis suddenly appeared? Travis, who had come of age years ago, but who had never tried to find him. He'd told Dillon not to forget, and then, apparently, had promptly forgotten Dillon.

But Dillon didn't forget. The only rationale he could contrive for Travis not contacting him was that Travis had given up on him, just like the rest of his family had.

When he pulled his thoughts from his ruminations, he saw the exit ramp for the airport and pulled through three lanes of blaring traffic and raced down the ramp. He needed someone to talk to; someone whose logic had never failed him. Only one other man beside Roland had lifted Dillon up and given him the courage to keep going. He needed to talk to Shu-shu.

***

Shu-shu was a Chinese immigrant who spoke very little English. But despite that, he'd built a bustling small business and raised his kids to believe they could do anything. He found Dillon feverish and incoherent behind the dumpster of his store only seven months after Dillon had been forced into the streets.

At almost seventeen, Dillon wasn't a small boy, but Shu-shu had picked him up like he was a child and brought him into his store, placing him on a cot he had in the back. Barking orders in Chinese to his wife and two kids, the man stripped Dillon of his clothing, wrapped him in a blanket, and fed him a soup that Dillon thought was the most amazing substance he'd ever tasted. He passed out shortly after.

When he awoke some days later, he expected to be in a hospital under lock and key waiting for the local sheriff or a case worker. They wouldn't have let him go until they determined his age and ran his background. But when he came to, he was still in Shu-shu's store. He tried to get up but couldn't. He was just too weak. He laid back down and let his eyes roam around, attempting to figure out where he was and how he'd gotten there. There were boxes everywhere, some in English, but most in Chinese. A gray metal desk overflowed with paperwork in the far corner and had some kind of thing with a bunch of beads on top of it. An abacus, he realized as his head cleared.

"The fuck?" he asked himself. He remembered nothing.

Shu-shu came to check on him a short time later. He smiled when he saw Dillon was awake and called out to his son, Bao.

Bao was round-faced and pimply and had an immediate dislike of Dillon. He was about a year or two younger than Dillon and gave off the distinct impression that Dillon had somehow stolen something from him already.

Shu-shu said something to him in Chinese and told the boy to interpret.

"Who are you and what do you want?" Bao sneered. Shu-shu cuffed him in the back of the head. Bao frowned and tried again. "My father would like to know your name."

"Frank," Dillon answered.

Shu-shu spoke to the boy again. "My father asks about your parents. He thinks you are not so long on the street."

Dillon looked down at the floor and shook his head. Shu-shu didn't need an interpreter for that. He spoke to his son again.

"My father says to rest and build your strength. He'll talk to you when you're better."

Hunter looked up at the man and nodded. He saw kindness in those eyes and an old misery which he couldn't put his finger on.

Bao, who called himself Kevin hoping he'd fit in better with his American peers, disappeared with a snide curl of his nose. His sister showed up soon after with another bowl of soup and some rice. She fed him while her father sat at the desk and did his paperwork.

She was a beautiful girl in her early teens who flashed her eyes at Dillon more than once. He smiled back but was still so tired that he just couldn't hold up to her girlish antics for long.

"What's your name?" Dillon asked.

"Ah-tam," she answered with a small smile. "It means like an orchid." She blushed after she said it and looked back at her father.

She was no orchid, Dillon thought. She was round and thick already. She wouldn't be one of those plastic looking Asian models you saw on TV. She was pretty, but she was going to be a big-boned woman.

He sipped at the soup. "Very good," he told her.

She beamed. "I made it."

"Where am I?" Dillon asked.

She explained where the store was located and how her father had found him behind the dumpster, likely on the verge of death. She said her father had used the old medicines on him and wouldn't call the police or a doctor, despite the nagging by her mother who was in the front of the store minding their customers. "She's still angry about the whole situation," Ah-tam informed him.

She went on and on until he couldn't take anymore chattering. He pushed the soup away. "What's your father's name?"

She turned and rattled off a few sentences he didn't understand. The man kept at what he was doing and answered over his shoulder.

"My father says you may call him Shu-shu."

"What's that mean?"

"Uncle," Ah-tam told him.

***

It hadn't been easy for him to leave Shu-shu's store. He would've worked for nothing if they'd let him use the cot. It was warm, he had food and Shu-shu genuinely seemed to like him. Ah-tam was infatuated, but both son and mother were adamantly opposed to Dillon being anywhere near them. When it finally came out that Dillon had been prostituting to survive, Shu-shu's wife had started screaming, calling him mài de, which Dillon quickly recognized as something less than flattering.

When he left, Shu-shu handed him several hundred dollars and a Chinese-English dictionary. "You learn," he said. And Dillon had, haltingly and in small segments. When he was desperate, when he couldn't find a trick or a place to put his head, he went back and waited to catch Shu-shu alone.

He didn't want to impose on Shu-shu's kindness or create problems with his family, but the streets had some dire days. He practiced his Chinese, got a bowl of soup, and used the cot for a few hours' rest. Then he went back to the streets again.

Two years later, Shu-shu's son was gunned down in a botched robbery attempt in the store. Shu-shu's wife never came back downstairs again. Only Shu-shu and Ah-tam maintained it afterward, and they welcomed him with open arms. Ah-tam had, by that time, gotten over her teenage infatuation and thought it was cool that she had a real gay friend. Apparently, he was unlike the little twinky boys she went to school with.

"They might need your friendship as much as I do, Ah-tam. Have you ever thought of that?" Dillon asked her one day as they organized the stock in the back room. "Just because they act like little insecure jerks doesn't mean they don't need a friend. It's usually the biggest indicator that they do."

She studied him for a moment and then nodded thoughtfully before checking to see if her father was around. "Do you know why my dad likes you?"

Dillon shook his head, hoping he wasn't about to hear that it had anything to do with sex.

She looked around the store again and lowered her voice. "His brother was gay. His parents drove him from the house and he died. I think he died in prison in China, but I don't know. He won't speak of it. Bao and I heard my parents arguing about it one night." She put her finger to her lips, swearing him to secrecy. But it was then that he understood the name Shu-shu had given him: zhizi, brother's son.

He felt a lump in his throat and looked down at the floor

wondering what would've happened to him if Shu-shu's parents hadn't sent their son out to die. It was basically what his own parents had done.

It was five more months before he met Roland and began to work for him.

***

But now, as Dillon pulled off the highway and up to the store, he thought about how Bao should be taking Shu-shu's place. Shu-shu looked old and nearly defeated. The storefront was as weather-beaten as the neighborhood which surrounded it.

Shu-shu raised his arms against the headlights, then smiled as he saw Dillon step out and come to the door. "Zhizi." He waved him inside and closed the door behind them. Bars rattled down over the windows and soon the two of them were standing in the shadows of the back room.

"How have you been?" Shu-shu asked him in Chinese.

"Good," Dillon answered. His gaze wandered around the store. It seemed like the place never changed.

"Zhizi."

Dillon brought his eyes back to Shu-shu.

"What do you need? Ask. I'm too old to let time slip away like this."

Dillon smiled. Shu-shu had been saying that since they'd met.

Shu-shu was as fully aware of Dillon's family situation as he was about Dillon's new financial status. Dillon kept him informed of everything important in his life and often sought him out for advice. He knew the things Dillon had gone through on the streets and he'd been the rock who Dillon had rested on when it all became too much. Roland had helped him financially with the escort service, but it was Shu-shu who had been his emotional stronghold.

"I've met someone," Dillon said as he started to explain his relationship with Hunter. He explained how they'd met, how he felt, and then the whirlwind of emotions which had erupted over Travis' sudden and possible reemergence in his life.

Shu-shu nodded and waved him to silence. He smiled as he wiggled his index finger at Dillon with a playful grin. "I knew what it was when I saw you."

"How?" Dillon asked skeptically.

Shu-shu gestured at the air around him. "It surrounds you, in your face, your eyes, and your stance. Loving someone gives you courage; being loved back gives you strength. I see both. It is nice to see it on you, finally."

"You think… He loves me?" Dillon asked as if the very question was mined.

Shu-shu smiled. "That is not for me to answer. But some part of you believes it."

"But my cousin, my family…"

Shu-shu looked at him curiously. "They have never left you, Zhizi. Not once. Tell me this isn't true."

Dillon shook his head. It was true. Dillon couldn't deny it, especially not to Shu-shu.

"Use the strength he gives you," Shu-shu said. "Look at the courage he gives you. Do you think your family could defeat that with their words? It is time to break with the past, Zhizi. You are a man now. They cannot overcome you with childish noises."

"So what should I do?" Dillon asked.

"Do?" Shu-shu repeated. "What you have always done, what was right for you right at that moment. Synchronicity brought you to this place in your life, which might be why your cousin and your lover have come at the same time. What you do with that moment..." He shrugged one shoulder. "That is also not for me to say."

Dillon frowned and looked at the floor. He never got a straight answer with Shu-shu. He always had to figure it out.

Shu-shu yawned loudly and stretched his arms out as he stood. "Now this old man must get to bed. Lock the door behind you."

Dillon watched as he started towards the stairs that led to the apartment above. In all the years since he'd known Shu-shu, Dillon had never been invited up to his home. It was his wife's way of reaffirming that he wasn't part of the family, no matter what Shu-shu decreed.

"Thank you," he said as Shu-shu started up the stairs.

Shu-shu turned slightly and nodded before he disappeared.

Chapter 16

Dillon went back out to his car and sat in the parking lot. He watched the windows above the store go out as Shu-shu went to bed. One of the curtains parted momentarily and he knew Shu-shu's wife must have peeked out at him.

He was still a non-person to her. When he tried to offer his condolences at Bao's funeral, she'd looked right through him as if he wasn't there and said absolutely nothing. He left the funeral thinking that was likely the same type of response he'd get from his own parents if he ever showed up in front of them again.

But wasn't that exactly what he was doing to himself now? Wasn't he making himself into a non-person once again? He was running from Hunter because he might bump into his family? Was that the message Shu-shu was trying to give him?

They hadn't been a part of his life for a decade and here he was throwing away a beautiful man because he was afraid to face them. If that were the case, then he should probably consider moving right now. Tonight. He could go somewhere out west or up north where he'd be sure they'd never bump into each other.

He could just take his money and go.

His lips pursed as he thought about it again, but he'd made that decision before he'd even met Hunter. He wasn't going to run off and start life over again based on a bunch of lies. And he damned sure wouldn't let his family push him around again. What had Shu-shu said? They couldn't overcome him with childish noises anymore?

"No," he said aloud, speaking ten years back. "You drove me away once. Not again." He started the car and jumped back on the interstate driving towards Hunter's apartment.

When he stopped in front of the building, he looked up and saw Hunter's lights still on. Looking down at his watch he did a double take. It was only ten-fifteen. Of course it was. Shu-shu closed at nine and opened at four AM for the commuters heading to the airport. Their dinner with Lydia had been early and...

He rolled his head back to the headrest and shut his eyes. With a loud sigh, he rubbed his hand across his face. Lydia was spending the night. "Shit!" he yelled, slamming his palms against the steering wheel in frustration.

He glanced at the windows again and wondered how Hunter had explained his sudden departure. Did he tell Lydia he was a prostitute? It didn't really matter. He'd seen the look on Hunter's face when he left. It was enough to know how pissed and hurt Hunter was.

Dillon couldn't blame him. He'd left Hunter right in the middle of dinner and blatantly lied and told him he was going to see a client. How much more of a slap in the face could there be than that? Oh, excuse me. I'm off to fuck someone else right now.

"You should've just fucking told him," Dillon barked at himself.

But, no. He shook his head at the thought. A few dinner dates and meeting mom didn't mean wanting a relationship in anyone's book. He was being allowed a slow introduction into the fold, and he'd already fucked it up by running away.

He propped his elbow on the door and stared out the driver's window. Maybe he was putting too much into this too soon. For all he knew, Hunter could've dragged a dozen men in front of Margie and Lydia. Maybe they vetted his flings. Dillon didn't know anything for sure.

But he hadn't seen that scenario reflected in Lydia's eyes, nor did he see it in Margie's, and she was probably the more likely of the two to be examining Hunter's boyfriends.

What he'd seen in both of them was interest and curiosity, not the rolling here we go again dismissal that typically sat behind the polite smile which that situation dictated.

He looked up at the apartment lights again. He had to apologize. He had to make Hunter understand how hard this was for him. Ten years of freezing his emotions to non-reaction had changed him and Hunter had thrown all that false poise into oblivion.

"Fuck," he mumbled, staring at his hands as they gripped the steering wheel. For the first time in many years, he understood how deeply his father's rejection affected his life. Not just his life on the street or in between the sheets, but how he interacted with people. He kept them distant, acting as the continually consummate professional whore he'd become.

He glanced up at Hunter's windows again. Did he want to put

Hunter through all the bullshit he still had to deal with within himself? Could he truly love someone and willingly subject them to that?

Tears started forming and he shook them off. No, I'm done with that, he told himself. Shu-shu was right. His family had taken enough. He looked at the windows again. Jesus, why is it so hard to say I need you?

He took a breath and stepped out of the car, his eyes locked on Hunter's windows. Lydia or no Lydia, he had to say something. He had to let Hunter know. He had to take the chance.

***

Hunter took another swig and grimaced. What the fuck was he doing? He wasn't a drinker. If he drank the whole bottle, he'd probably end up dead, in the hospital, or puking his guts out for the next three days. He capped it and put it on the table beside him, not even a quarter of it gone.

The likelihood that it was going to help how he felt right now was slim to fucking none anyway. The first time he and Dillon had sex, he'd kept the sheets on the bed for three days afterward. He'd kept the traces of Dillon's presence close to him so that when he curled up at night he wouldn't feel so fucking alone. How pathetic was that?

No wonder Dillon had gone racing out of the restaurant. He never claimed he was going to give anything up for Hunter, and Hunter had never asked. Hunter had assumed.

So why the fuck had that call hurt so much?

There was no understandable answer to his question other than that he was obviously and illogically in desperate need of this guy. He wouldn't call it love yet, but it was pretty damned close. And that didn't make a bit of sense.

What did love look like? He wondered. Did sighted people have an advantage in that department? When he was a kid, he'd always heard the other children talking about a look or what people were wearing or the some other outward visual signs of affection he couldn't witness. And everything he'd ever read always spoke about that glow in someone's eyes, that longing that couldn't be forgotten. What did Dillon see when he looked at him? A blank? A question mark? All Hunter ever wanted was to be treated like an ordinary person, to be loved and to love. He wasn't asking for special treatment, he just wanted what everyone else wanted. Not to be alone.

The first time he'd been to bed with Dillon, Hunter had just wanted to fuck. He wanted a body next to him that made more noise than the sound of a hot vibrator.

But after that... After that, he'd wanted more. He still wanted more. He couldn't help it. He knew it wasn't logical, but nothing about this had been sensible from the start. They fucked a few times and they went out for dinner once. Dillon met Margie and his mom, but nowhere in any of those casual interactions was the word relationship written.

They had the physical aspect of it down pat, but the rest... There was no rest and that was the problem. His problem was that he'd been wishing for what wasn't intended or meant to be.

He rubbed at his temples, a headache swelling from the vodka already.

He hadn't expected this when Dillon propositioned him on the street. None of it, and maybe he wasn't prepared for it either. Maybe that was the problem right there. Not that Dillon was a prostitute, but that he couldn't handle the reality of it. He couldn't adjust to the fact that Dillon's job was to bed other men as desperate as he was.

The downstairs buzzer sounded and he snapped his head in the direction of the intercom. "Mom," he gasped. He'd completely forgotten about her.

He shook his head at his stupidity and started to get up and then paused. Checking his watch, he realized over an hour had passed since she'd dropped him off. She had to have driven home already. She had her own key anyway, she didn't need the buzzer. And since Dillon was getting his brains fucked out by some client, it meant it had to be one of his ignorant fucking neighbors again.

"Find your key, you asshole," he yelled at the intercom.

But it persisted, a loud irritating shrill which pulsated and then would not abate. Whoever was down there laid on the button and would not let up.

Instantly, he was enraged and stomped over to the panel. He was going to go down there and stomp this asshole all over the fucking hallway. "You better not be down there when I come down, you fucking asshole, or I'm going to kill you!" he screamed into the mic.

There was silence. "It's me," Dillon answered, a hesitancy in his voice.

Hunter froze, his breath and his anger gone. He pushed the buzzer and flung the door to his apartment open. He heard Dillon pound up the stairs and then felt him burst into his arms. He squeezed. He squeezed and didn't let go.

***

Hunter ran his hand across Dillon's chest, down to his belly and brought it back up again. He rubbed his finger across Dillon's nipple and toyed with it as he considered how their relationship had grown in such a short time. He wanted to know more about Dillon, much more. He wanted to know why he was so reserved when that trait seemed so at odds with his livelihood. He wanted to know why he was so secretive about his past, which obviously had something to do with him becoming a prostitute. Most of all he wanted to know if he planned on getting out of the trade. That was really the foremost of Hunter's questions.

Dillon had come back to him tonight, but could they build on that? Would he come back tomorrow or the next day? And would he understand that Hunter wasn't willing to share him with someone else? Because as much as he'd like to claim that he was an open person, Hunter knew that Dillon's job would always interfere with any potential they had between them. Hunter understood that now more than ever. There was no way around how he felt about it.

But did he have a right to demand that Dillon quit? Wouldn't

Dillon flinch at such a requirement? Wouldn't he if he were in Dillon's shoes? And was he willing to risk asking Dillon and possibly losing him over it?

He sighed in frustration. If there was one thing he'd learned from working with writers, it was that words only came when they were ready to come. You couldn't force them, not if you wanted honesty. And basically the words he wanted to hear from Dillon were words of commitment. He could fantasize and rationalize about it any way he wanted to. But essentially he'd be asking Dillon to give up everything. If that wasn't the ultimate definition of commitment, then he didn't know what was. No ring involved, just give up your whole fucking life.

Up until tonight, he'd only toyed with the idea of turning their sexual escapades into a relationship. But it had always been this aching and unreachable fantasy since their first tryst. As much as he thought he'd wished it were true, he'd never honestly considered it a real possibility. It had always been just a flight of romantic fiction. Not so now. Not after the pain he felt sitting in the restaurant hearing Dillon say goodbye.

Now he realized that he did want something long term with Dillon. Or, if not long term, at least something more meaningful – something beyond the sex and the few shared moments they'd had with each other so far.

He stopped playing with Dillon's nipple and put his hand flat on Dillon's chest, feeling his heartbeat and his breath. He loved this closeness, the fact that Dillon didn't seem to mind that he liked to touch him constantly.

"You okay?" Dillon asked.

"Yeah, why do you ask?"

He felt Dillon shrug. They hadn't spoken when he came in. They'd clasped and joined and then come to the bedroom and melted into each other. But neither of them had said anything about what happened or why he'd come back.

Wait, Hunter told himself. Let him make the choice. Don't force it. He has to be the one, I can't demand it. "I was just thinking what a hot body you had. And how lucky I was that Margie and I had an argument," Hunter replied. He wanted Dillon to explain how he'd come to be in his bed, instead of in a client's.

"What if I had been fat?" Dillon asked, a smile blossoming in his voice. "Some big old hairy troll looking for a quick fuck?"

"I would've kicked your ass to the curb in a minute," Hunter told him, the sudden burst of humor making his thoughts lighter.

Dillon laughed.

"What's so funny? Blind people can discriminate too. It's not pure love and all that bullshit about it not being based on your looks. We do have our own tastes and pet peeves too," Hunter informed him.

Dillon laughed playfully at Hunter's indignation. "Okay, I get it. But how did you know what I would look like without touching me first?" Dillon asked.

Hunter ran his hand across Dillon's body again, the curve and strength of him was absolutely unmistakable. "You didn't rasp like someone who was overweight, and your step wasn't as heavy. It's pretty easy to tell the difference. Someone who's hefty but muscular breathes a lot different from someone who's overweight. Too many more of those cigarettes, though, and even I might not be able to tell the difference."

"I'm hefty?" Dillon asked.

Hunter gently slapped him on his stomach. "Not you, it's an example."

"But isn't that like discriminating against you because you're blind?" Dillon asked.

"Yup, and I don't give a fuck. They don't want to fuck me because I'm blind, fine. I don't want fatties in my bed. I am allowed to have someone according to my own tastes, aren't I?"

"But big girls have more fun," Dillon argued.

"But they also get to choose," Hunter countered. "They don't just drop their panties for any asshole that comes along."

"True," Dillon conceded.

Hunter realized they were avoiding what they needed to talk about. But maybe it was their best option. Maybe just being together and holding each other would allow them to calm the emotions the phone call had brought forth.

Dillon nuzzled against Hunter's ear and slid his hand down to slip through the weave of Hunter's pubic hair. "So you were happy that we met?"

Hunter heard the caution in his voice and tilted his head. He arched his back as Dillon took a firm grasp at the base of his cock and began a desperately slow massage. "Well, you're housebroken anyway," Hunter muttered, pushing his growing cock deeper against Dillon's hand.

Dillon nipped at his earlobe and pulled his hand away.

"Ow," Hunter yelped, rubbing his ear and feeling the small imprints of Dillon's teeth. "You bit me."

"I think I might need a little more training," Dillon growled.

Hunter pushed up against him, letting Dillon feel the heat of his length as he reached for Dillon's nipple and gave it a sharp but lasting twist. "Are you sure about that?" he asked, holding the nipple in his fingers.

He heard Dillon wince and suck the air in through his teeth before he answered. "Yes."

"The bruise on your hip the first time we met, what was it from?" Hunter demanded suddenly, his voice raw with the many things he wanted to know about and do to Dillon.

Dillon was curling into Hunter's grasp trying to alleviate some of the pain in his nipple. But when Hunter reached down and grabbed his nuts and started twisting them slowly in the opposite direction, he had no place to go. "Client," he hissed.

Hunter was starting to hate that fucking word.

"Do you like the pain?" Hunter asked him, slowly twisting his nipple as he released his nuts and slid his fingers up to the tip of Dillon's now rock hard cock.

"Sometimes," Dillon yelped at the mixture of pleasure and pain.

Hunter smiled and leaned in close. All his dark fantasies crept forward. His insecurities took a back seat as lust came up on him. He licked at the salty sweat on Dillon's chest, not quite sure if he wanted to share his darker kink with someone who wasn't one hundred percent his. "Someday, you might learn what my name is really about," he whispered as he let Dillon's nipple go.

"Please…" Dillon begged, the rush of endorphins making him whimper.

"Not now. Turn over," Hunter instructed as he rose.

***

Dillon grabbed the back of Hunter's neck. He pulled himself up and pressed his lips to him, their tongues dancing a hot pirouette around each other. To hear the aggressive attitude in Hunter's needy demand made him hot. He'd been both dominant top and submissive bottom through the years and had enjoyed both roles. But enjoying the role wasn't the same as giving yourself entirely to it, and he'd yet to do that with anyone.

Hunter pushed him away. "Enough, turn over."

Dillon rolled onto his stomach and opened his legs as Hunter pushed the sheets down and knelt between them. When Hunter came forward and stretched across Dillon's back, he could feel the tip of Hunter's cock resting gently at his hole. He started sliding backwards, hoping to capture it and put it fully inside of him. But Hunter had other plans.

"You like that?" Hunter asked, his tongue curling around the shell of Dillon's ear as he gave a small forward thrust.

"Mm, yes. I want you inside me," Dillon moaned.

***

Hunter huffed in Dillon's intoxicating fragrance and started nibbling. His tongue became a hot, insurgent little prod, moving and tasting as it slipped over the top of Dillon's ear and down the soft, delicate skin behind it. He started inching down Dillon's body, licking, rubbing, sucking, and luxuriating in his sexual perfume – that foreign, tangy spice Dillon threw off. "Beautiful," he murmured as he made his way down Dillon's spine with small butterfly kisses.

He clamped his teeth down on the left globe of Dillon's ass, leaving his mark and drawing a little blood as Dillon yelped. "You're marked now," he told Dillon before he slipped down further. He put his hands under Dillon's pelvis and lifted his ass from the bed.

Dillon came up willingly, moving his legs slightly forward to give himself some leverage. Hunter licked and sucked his way around the beautiful piece of sculpted manhood he had in his hands until he got to its center. Then he plunged his hot tongue into Dillon's now quivering hole.

A long intake of breath was all Hunter heard before Dillon started moaning and thrusting his ass back. "All the way up," Hunter commanded, digging his tongue in deeper as Dillon rose to all fours.

"Uhh, don't…stop," Dillon pleaded as his hand snaked down and started tugging at his throbbing cock.

Hunter started from the bottom of his balls and licked up in a long, slow stroke until his tongue came to the end of Dillon's spine.

He did it twice more before he rested his chin on Dillon's back and whispered up to him. "Shh," he said to Dillon's whimpers.

He had no plans to stop. He was lost in Dillon's ripe man-scent. He slid his hand underneath Dillon and felt the weight of his balls when he rolled them in his palm. He swatted Dillon's groping hand away and went back to rimming his hole as he continued to fondle them. He loved this ass. Loved it and could not get enough of it. He pulled Dillon's cheeks apart with the fingers of his free hand and pushed his tongue in further, laving and licking as Dillon pushed himself back against his face.

He took his hand away and let Dillon's cheeks trap his tongue as he reached down and massaged Dillon's cock and balls with both hands. He jerked him slowly, gently caressing and tugging as his tongue teased out Dillon's pleasured grunts. When Dillon relaxed back into the myriad sensations, Hunter grabbed his sack and pulled down in a quick, sharp jerk as his tongue plunged deep into Dillon's puckered entrance. He smiled when he heard Dillon gasp in electrified shock.

Snatching Dillon's cock, he folded it down so that it was exposed to him before he began licking it with short strokes of his tongue. He wrapped his lips around the head, brushing it gently as Dillon cooed above him. He moved from Dillon's manhood to his hole and back again, keeping Dillon's cock pressed firmly against his taint so that it forced his nuts apart and made Dillon ache to be bathed with his hot tongue.

Hunter moaned loudly and deliberately as he took Dillon's

cock deeper into his mouth. He let the vibrations drive Dillon slightly wild while his thumb plunged into Dillon's musky hole. He inhaled Dillon's fragrance again, sunk his thumb in deep, and listened to Dillon moan as he sucked his freely flowing pre-cum.

"You taste so good. I could lick your ass for hours," Hunter told him as he let go of Dillon's cock and took another swipe at his hole. He heard Dillon's cock swing forward and hit his hard stomach with a thwap. He smiled, plunged his tongue into Dillon one last time, and then got on his knees and put his cockhead at Dillon's entrance.

"You want this?" he asked Dillon as he grabbed his hips.

"Yes…please," Dillon pleaded, pushing himself back against Hunter.

Hunter slid in a fraction of an inch, teasing Dillon as he bent over and began kissing his back. When he straightened up again, he took a firm grip on Dillon's waist and slammed himself into Dillon's ass, filling him completely in one thrust. He loved the power of doing that, loved that Dillon's ass clenched when he first pushed against his hole, then opened in welcome and then re-clenched when he'd buried himself.

***

Dillon gasped as every muscle in his body suddenly went rigid with the luscious invasion. "Yes," he cried. "Yes, harder." He could feel the throbbing manhood that filled him. Hunter's balls were tight against his ass. He moaned as Hunter rubbed his cheeks with those hard, hard fingers, pinching and squeezing as if he were waiting for something.

Dillon started moving, wanting the motion, the friction, and the heat of Hunter's fat cock.

"No," Hunter snapped, slapping him on the ass and tightening his grip on his hips.

Hunter's cock was throbbing inside of him. He could feel the small pulses Hunter was using as he twitched his cock in Dillon's ass. It was just barely rubbing against his prostate, but it was driving him crazy, making him beg without any words. It was pure pleasure.

Then without a word or indication, Hunter dug his nails into Dillon's ass cheeks. He pulled his cock completely out and rammed back in again, beginning a long dicked thrusting fuck that made Dillon scream in pleasure.

***

Hunter rode Dillon hard, panting and thrusting until he felt Dillon's ass start to spasm around his cock. "So fucking hot," he screamed as he dug his fingers into Dillon's flesh and dragged his body up and down his long shaft.

When he heard Dillon moan and smelled the aroma of his hot spunk hitting the sheets, he couldn't do anything but dump his load deep in Dillon's ass. He slammed and thrust into him like he wanted to push his whole body inside.

His final thrust pushed both of them forward and he collapsed on Dillon's back as the last of his cum sprayed into Dillon and flooded him with his seed. He inhaled Dillon's scent again as he kissed at his temple and brought his hands up underneath Dillon's shoulders. His cock was still lodged deep inside as he lay on his sweaty, breathless partner.

He knew right then there was no way he was going to give Dillon up willingly. It wasn't just because the sex was hot. It was that it was erotically intimate, as if they were two intricate pieces which fit together as one.

Neither of them could move. They lay there, breathing with each other, breathing into each other.

***

"I quit," Dillon finally mumbled.

"What?"

Dillon rolled Hunter off and then crawled back on top of his body. He slid his ass back onto Hunter's still hard cock before it could go soft and then lay down on his chest. He didn't want to give it up so fast and smiled at how insatiable Hunter really was.

"I said I quit. I'm quitting. No more hustling. No more escort service."

He felt Hunter freeze beneath him and was hit by an instant and intense jolt of despair. Hunter's body language made it obvious that he didn't want a relationship with a prostitute and now he'd all but announced that he was leaving the profession for him.

Stupid, fucking stupid, he told himself, his chest filling with emotion. There were probably a hundred things running through Hunter's mind right now, all of them hot realizations about Dillon's trade.

He dislodged himself from Hunter's cock and started getting

off the bed. "Sorry, I didn't mean to imply…"

"Shut up," Hunter said with force.

He reached up and quickly found Dillon's shoulders and jerked him back down. "Please be quiet," he whispered. "I don't want you to go anywhere."

Dillon looked at him in shock. When his astonishment was gone, only a second or two, he felt the warmth of Hunter's words run through his body like a sunrise and gently kissed his lips. "I don't want to be with anyone else anymore," he confided to Hunter when he pulled away. He knew deep within himself that this was, at last, an accurate statement. It wasn't a question. It wasn't fear talking. It was his heart.

"And I don't want you to be either," Hunter told him. "I want you with me, and only with me."

"But my past…"

"I don't give a shit about that," Hunter admonished him immediately. "It brought you to me. That's all I care about. I want you, now, here, just as you are."

"Things could get…awkward," Dillon warned.

"My whole fucking life is awkward. It's always been. My question to you is why are you making excuses when I can hear what you want in your voice just as much as I want it? I don't know how it happened or why, but I can't pretend anymore. You almost broke me in half when you left the restaurant tonight."

Dillon was quiet for a moment, feeling sixteen again, feeling like he was sitting on the edge of a precipice about to jump off and not knowing where, or if, he'd land. But when he looked at Hunter laying there, his hard body, his harder love, he knew that this was someone who would not willingly give him up. Hunter wouldn't toss him aside, not for anything or anyone.

And instead of answering with words he reached forward, closed his eyes, and found Hunter's mouth, letting it say all the words that his fears had never let him express before.

THE END

What happens next with Dillon and Hunter?
Find out in
Afflicted II.

About the Author

Award-winning writer BRANDON SHIRE is a distinct voice in contemporary LGBT fiction. Mr. Shire was chosen as a Top Read in 2011, Best in LGBTQ Fiction for 2011 & 2012 and garnered several Honorable Mentions, as well as a Rainbow Award for Best Gay Contemporary Fiction. He resides in the South.

You can find out more at BrandonShire.com.

Other books by Brandon Shire

The Love of Wicked Men

Sid Rivers and Jack Brown are two sides of the same coin. One is a lawyer with his own firm and dreams of money and power; the other is a criminal with a lengthy record and a quest for vengeance. When they meet, sparks fly. But was their meeting an accident? Or was it planned by the billionaires who want to control their destiny?

The Love of Wicked Men is an erotic journey into the underbelly of the legal profession, the corporate culture of profit-at-any-cost, and the secret world of industrial espionage.

Cold – Gay Romance Series

Prison is a brutal, heartless, and demeaning environment. No one knows this better than a man sentenced to life in prison for murder. Lem Porter has given up, but when he finally meets someone who captures his heart, he soon realizes that there is more to life than just the walls which surround him.

AWARD-WINNING LITERARY LGBT FICTION:

Summer Symphony

A bisexual father loses his daughter to stillbirth and has no mechanism to cope until one man comes along and shows him the power of music, and the strength of a father's love.

Listening to Dust

When love blossoms unexpectedly and is then ripped away, a world shatters and a man with it. (RAINBOW AWARD WINNER)

The Value of Rain

Chronicle's one young man's journey into the world of 'reparative therapy' and reveals the destructive nature of families, secrets, and revenge. (BEST IN LGBTQ FICTION 2011).

Manufactured by Amazon.ca
Bolton, ON